The
Golf
Book
OF Lists

Everything Golf—From the Greatest Courses and Most Challenging Greens, to the Greatest Players and the Best Equipment

The Golf Book ᴏꜰ Lists

by Mitch Kaplan

New Page Books
A Division of Career Press, Inc.
Franklin Lakes, NJ

The Golf Book of Lists

Cover design by Fanzone Design Solutions
Printed in the U.S.A. by Book-mart Press
Edited by Dianna Walsh
Typeset by John J. O'Sullivan

To order this title, please call toll-free 1-800-CAREER-1
(NJ and Canada: 201-848-0310)
to order using VISA or MasterCard,
or for further information on books from Career Press.

The Career Press, Inc., 3 Tice Road, PO Box 687
Franklin Lakes, NJ 07417
www.careerpress.com
www.newpagebooks.com

Library of Congress Cataloging-in-Publication Data

Kaplan, Mitch.
    The golf book of lists : everything golf, from the greatest courses and the most challenging greens, to the greatest players and the best equipment / Mitch Kaplan.
      p.cm.
    Includes bibliographical references and index.
    ISBN 1-56414-483-6 (pbk.)
      1. Golf—Miscellanea. I. Title

GV967 .K26 2001
796.352—dc21

                         2001030328

Dedication

In memory of my father, Len, who instilled in me a love of sport.

Acknowledgments

Special thanks must be given to Mike Lewis, acquisitions editor, who tracked me down and gave me an offer I couldn't refuse. And, as always, thanks to my wife, Penny, who manages to stick by me in all these crazy projects.

Contents

Contents

Section 1

General

Highlights in Golf History

G olf history, of course, dates back to almost the Middle Ages, depending upon exactly whose account of things you want to believe. But, as Americans, we think the following dates hold significance. There are lots of other important dates, obviously, but there's a limit to how long this book can be.

25 Highlights in American Golf History

1. 1894

The Amateur Golf Association of the United States forms on December 22. Charter members are Newport Golf Club, Shinnecock Hills Golf Club, the Country Club (Brookline, Massachusetts), St. Andrew's Golf Club (Yonkers, New York), and the Chicago Golf Club. The name will soon be changed to the United States Golf Association (USGA), which will grow to be the governing body of golf throughout the United States. The organization stages its first U.S. amateur championship at Newport Golf Club the following year, won by Charles B. Macdonald The first U.S. Open, a distinctly secondary tournament, is held the very next day at the same site. Horace Rawlins wins in a field of 11; the top prize is $150. Later the first U.S. Women's amateur championship is won by Mrs. Charles S. Brown at the Meadow Brook Club in Hempstead, New York.

2. 1898

The wound-rubber golf ball is patented by Coburn Haskell and Bertram Work. It travels much farther than the traditional gutta-percha ball. Eight years later (1906), Englishman William Taylor patents the dimple-design golf-ball cover.

3. 1916

The Professional Golfers' Association of America—the PGA—is founded on April 10 in New York. It boasts 82 members. The organization stages its first tournament in October at Siwanoy Country Club in Bronxville, New York, where James M. Barnes defeats Jock Hutchinson 1-up. PGA membership reaches 23,000 in the year 2000.

4. 1922

The first Walker Cup Match takes place at National Golf Links of America in Southampton, New York. All countries are invited to compete, but only the United States and Great Britain take up the challenge. The United States wins.

5. 1924

The USGA sanctions the use of steel-shafted clubs.

6. 1927

The first Ryder Cup Matches are played. The United States defeats Great Britain 9.5 to 2.5 at the Worcester (Massachusetts) Country Club.

7. 1930

Bobby Jones wins the Grand Slam in a single year, which at that time consists of the USGA Open, USGA Amateur, British Open, and British Amateur. He promptly retires at age 28.

8. 1932

The first Curtis Cup Match is played. American women amateurs defeat the British 5.5 to 3.5.

9. 1941

The PGA opens the Golf Hall of Fame. First inductees are Willie Anderson, Tommy Armour, Jim Barnes, Chick Evans, Walter Hagen, Bobby Jones, John McDermott, Francis Ouimet, Gene Sarazen, Alex Smith, Jerry Travers, and Walter Travis.

10. 1951

After much haggling, the USGA and the Royal and Ancient Academy in Britain agree on a uniform Rules of Golf to be effected worldwide.

11. 1954

The U.S. Open is televised nationally for the first time, thrusting it into the forefront among major tournaments.

Bobby Jones (left) receiving a trophy from USGA president, W. C. Downes

12. 1954

Babe Zaharias returns to the LPGA Tour following cancer surgery and wins the U.S. Women's Open.

13. 1963

Arnold Palmer is the first player to surpass $100,000 in earnings in a single year.

14. 1971

Jack Nicklaus is the first professional to win the modern Grand Slam—the Masters, U.S. Open, British Open, and PGA Championship—twice.

15. 1971

Astronaut Alan Shephard smacks what must be the most famous golf shot ever when he plays on the moon.

16. 1973

The graphite club shaft is introduced.

17. 1976

The USGA adopts the Overall Distance Standard for golf balls, limiting them to 280 yards under standard test conditions. (And you wondered why you can't hit the ball 400 yards?)

18. 1979

TaylorMade introduces its first metal wood. (But, you still can't hit the ball 400 yards.)

19. 1980

Tom Watson is the first golfer to earn $500,000 in prize money in a single season.

20. 1980

The PGA Senior Tour begins; four official events are played, including the U.S. Senior Open.

21. 1981

Kathy Whitworth becomes the first woman to earn $1 million in career prize money.

22. 1990

Some 38 years after the USGA, Britain's Royal and Ancient Golf Club adopts the 1.68-inch diameter ball. For the first time since 1910, the Rules of Golf are standardized worldwide.

23. 1991

Oversized metal woods are introduced, and Callaway Golf's Big Bertha driver becomes one of the biggest-selling clubs of all time.

24. 1996

Tiger Woods wins his third consecutive U.S. Amateur title.

25. 2000

Tiger Woods breaks the $9 million mark for one year's winnings in tournament play.

50 International Golf History Highlights

There's some debate as to when this game was actually invented. More likely, it evolved. But it came to prominence and was made into something resembling its current form in Scotland, spreading from there to the worldwide pastime that it is today. Dating to the Middle Ages, here are 50 significant moments in golf's world history.

1. 1353

Historians point to this year as the first known reference to "chole," a game played in Belgium (a.k.a. Flanders) and thought to be the likely precursor to golf.

2. 1421

Golf is introduced to Scotland after a Scottish regiment allied with the French against the English is introduced to chole at the Siege of Bauge. Three men—Hugh Kennedy, Robert Stewart, and John Smale—are credited with bringing the game to Scotland.

3. 1457

Golf and football are banned by the Scottish Parliament of James II because they interfere with military training for the wars against England.

4. 1502

The Treaty of Glasgow is signed with England, and the Scottish ban on golf is ended.

James IV reputedly makes the first purchase of golf equipment, a set of clubs he acquires from a bow maker in Perth, Scotland.

5. 1527

The first known commoner golfer, Sir Robert Maule, is reported to have played on Barry Links, near the modern-day Carnoustie.

6. 1552

Golf is reputed to have first been played at St. Andrews.

7. 1567

Mary, Queen of Scots, is the first known female golfer. Mary, who was French, is also credited with introducing the game to France while she studied there and with coining the term "caddie," a name she gave to her helpers, who were known as cadets.

8. 1618

The feathery ball is invented.

Mary, Queen of Scots,
first female golfer

9. 1641

While Charles II plays at Leith, news of the Irish rebellion reaches him, thus beginning the English Civil War. He finishes his round.

10. 1642

John Dickson receives a license as official ball maker for Aberdeen, Scotland.

11. 1682

The first recorded international golf match. The Duke of York and John Paterstone of Scotland defeat two English noblemen at Leith.

12. 1744

The Honourable Company of Edinburgh Golfers is formed at Leith links. It is the first golf club.

13. 1754

The first codified Rules of Golf is published by the St. Andrews Golfers, which later becomes the Royal and Ancient Golf Club.

14. 1759

The first known stroke-play golf is played at St. Andrews. Previously, all golf was match-play.

15. 1764

The first four holes at St. Andrews are combined into two, reducing the round from 22 holes to 18 and creating the first 18-hole golf course.

16. 1766

The Blackheath Club is the first golf club outside of Scotland.

17. 1768

The first golf clubhouse is built at Leith.

18. 1810

A competition at Musselburgh is the first known reference to a women's golf contest.

19. 1820

The Bangalore Club is formed in India, the first club outside of the British Isles.

20. 1826

Hickory, imported to the British Isles from America, is first used to make golf shafts.

21. 1829

The North Berwick Club is founded, and it becomes the first to include women in its activities. They are not, however, permitted to play in competitions.

22. 1833

King William IV confers the distinction of "Royal" on the Perth Golfing Society. Royal Perth is thus the first Club to hold the distinction.

23. 1834

King William IV confers the title "Royal and Ancient" on the Golf Club at St. Andrews.

24. 1856

The Royal Curragh Golf Club is founded at Kildare, the first golf club in Ireland.

The Pau Golf Club is founded in France, the first on the European continent.

25. 1859

The first British Amateur Championship is won by George Condie of Perth.

26. 1861

The British Open begins, first won by Old Tom Morris.

27. 1867

The Ladies' Golf Club at St. Andrews is founded. It is the first golf club for women.

28. 1869

Young Tom Morris, age 17, wins the first of four successive British Open championships.

29. 1873

The Royal Montreal Golf Club is formed, the first club in Canada.

30. 1885

The Royal Cape Golf Club is founded at Wynberg, South Africa, the first club in Africa.

31. 1890

John Ball, an English amateur, becomes the first non-Scotsman and first amateur to win the British Open.

32. 1892

Gate money is charged for the first time at a match between Douglas Rollard and Jack White at Cambridge. It is used, for the first time, instead of private betting money, to stake the winning purse.

The Amateur Golf Championship of India and the East is instituted, the first international championship event.

33. 1893

The British Ladies' Golf Union is founded and its first Open Championship is won by Lady Margaret Scott.

34. 1894

The British Open is played on an English course for the first time and is won for the first time by an Englishman, J.H. Taylor.

35. 1900

Golf is confirmed as a global sport when it becomes an Olympic sport. It's the only time golf is included in the Games.

36. 1905

Women golfers from Great Britain and the United States play an international match. The British win six matches to one.

37. 1907

Arnaud Massey becomes the first European golfer to win the British Open.

38. 1908

Mrs. Gordon Robertson becomes the first female professional golfer.

39. 1913

The first professional international team match is played between teams from France and the United States at La Boulie, France.

40. 1914

Formation of The Tokyo Club at Komozawa launches Japanese golf.

41. 1922

Walker Cup Matches are instituted.

42. 1927

The inaugural Ryder Cup Matches are played between Britain and the United States.

43. 1932

The first Curtis Cup Matches are held at Wentworth in England.

44. 1933

Craig Wood hits a 430-yard drive at the Old Course's fifth hole during the British Open; it remains the longest drive ever hit in a major championship.

45. 1953

The Canada Cup is instituted, the first event to bring together teams from all over the world. After 1966, the tournament is known as the World Cup.

46. 1954

Peter Thomson becomes the first Australian to win a major tournament with a victory in the British Open.

47. 1977

Tom Watson defeats Jack Nicklaus by one stroke in the British Open at Turnberry. As they were tied after both the second and third rounds, and paired with each other during the final 36 holes, many consider this to be the most exciting tournament ever.

48. 1979

The Ryder Cup expands from a British Isles team to a European team.

49. 1990

The Royal and Ancient Golf Club, after 38 years, adopts the 1.68-inch diameter ball, and for the first time since 1910, the Rules of Golf are standardized throughout the world.

50. 1992

Two men—Simon Clough and Boris Janic—complete 18-hole rounds in five countries in one day, walking each course. They play in France, Luxembourg, Belgium, Holland, and Germany, completing the epic in 16 hours and 35 minutes.

7 Damned Good Reasons to Play Golf

1. A round of golf provides both physical and mental exercise.

True, the physical aspect of golf isn't too strenuous and, if you're circling the course in a cart, it could never be mistaken for an aerobic workout. It's also true that the mental side of the game often proves more demonic than pensive, bringing out any devil that may be lurking below your sanguine, circumspect, surface personality. But, still, a round is healthy (for those in control of their emotions) and safe (for those who can play at a comfortable pace), and surely few pastimes are more invigorating than a handful of hours spent walking the links with good friends in the fresh air, especially if you're five holes up and playing for $150 a hole.

2. Golf offers marvelous social benefits.

Can you think of a better way to hang out with your friends or to make new ones? Can you think of a better way to schmooze with the boss or that key client? Can you think of a better way to escape the real world while creating and sharing a common bond with your peers? You can? Then, trade in your clubs and go do it.

3. Few pastimes afford such an excellent, albeit elusive, chance to answer personal challenges and meet goals.

Some of us aim to lower our handicap. Others aim to eliminate it altogether and become a scratch player. For still others, the ultimate achievement is to shoot a par round. Many strive to shoot par on their home or favorite course. And, then again, some of us are still battling to hit two good shots in a row. No matter what your personal Holy Grail, the game provides an incredibly uplifting sense of individual achievement when, if ever, these goals are achieved.

4. Golf creates a marvelous excuse to travel.

Some folks go to Italy to hear the great operas at La Scala. Golfers can travel to the far corners of the Earth to prove that shanking shots is an international language understood no matter what the local tongue may be.

5. Golf is good for the soul because it brings you closer to nature.

Well, sort of. You do play outdoors. Often in beautiful settings. And, in some places wildlife actually gets in your way. (Check the local rules when playing a lie that's dangerously close to an alligator, rhino, or sleeping stray dog.)

6. Golf teaches life lessons.

You learn to answer challenges, perform under pressure, concentrate, and, perhaps, handle frustration. You might also learn diplomacy, and at what point diplomacy breaks down; your personal breaking point; financial management (how many balls can I afford to invest in today?); and hunting and gathering skills while searching for balls lost in the woods.

7. This is a life sport.

You should only live so long to master it!

5 Very Gauche Breaches of Golf Etiquette

1. Do not invite following golfers to play through if you are holding them up.

Why should you? Who are they anyway? Just because they are (pick one) better, faster, bigger, stronger, wiser, or more influential than you, do they deserve to play through?

2. Do not replace the flagstick properly before leaving the green.

Joe said he'd get that, didn't he?

3. Do not replace your divots.

Did *I* do that?

4. Do not create a disturbance while others are shooting.

Do quarterbacks whimper when the crowd breaks the noise meter? Does a pitcher refuse to throw because the third base coach is insulting his mother? Why is it that only tennis, golf, and chess require such silence and courtesy?

5. Do not pretend you didn't really make contact with the ball on that shot deep in the rough.

Nobody saw you, anyway, except maybe the good Lord…and your conscience. But you can't have any conscience. If you did, you'd be home doing yard chores.

4

7 Excellent Reasons Not to Play Golf

1. Keep your sanity.
2. Keep your self-esteem.
3. Keep your money.
4. Keep your time free for better things.
5. Keep starvation from your door.
6. Keep your friends.
7. Keep your marriage.

No golf for me, thanks. I'm trying to quit.

5

The Many Components of the Golf Swing

ed Williams once said that hitting a baseball was the single hardest thing to do in all of sport. He was probably correct. But, hitting a golf ball successfully is probably the single most frustrating thing to do in all of sport. Certainly, hitting it well twice in a row is a feat worthy of publicity and headlines on your personal Web site.

On the surface of it, the golf swing should be a simple act. But when you break it down into its component parts, you begin to see just what a miracle it is that anyone ever hits the ball where he/she wants it to go. In the following list, I break the swing down into a mere 50 elements. When you think of the swing in these terms, you no longer wonder why your ball is always in the water or, worse, behind you.

1. Select a club.
2. Address the ball.
3. Set your feet.
4. Relax.
5. Bend the knees slightly.
6. Grip the club. Don't choke it; don't chuck it.
7. Site your shot (or, look where you're going to hit it).

8. Relax.

9. Ripple the fingers and check on grip alignment.

10. Site the ball (or, look at it).

11. Site the shot. Again.

12. Site the ball. Again.

13. Straighten the back.

14. Loosen the shoulders.

15. Relax.

16. Begin the backswing, while...

17. ...bending the front knee down and inwards, while...

18. ...keeping the front arm straight, while...

19. ...bending the back elbow, and....

20. ...keeping the head down, so that...

21. ...you can site the ball, and...

22. ...stay relaxed, and...

23. ...arc the club parallel to your stance and target, while...

24. ...twisting the hips, until...

25. ...the swing apexes (front arm still straight), and...

26. ...cock the wrists.

27. Begin the downswing, while...

28. ...keeping the front arm straight, while...

29. ...swiveling the hips, and...

30. ...driving the shoulders forward, as you...

31. ...relax, and...

32. ...keep the head down, and...

33. ...shift the weight towards the front foot, as you...

34. ...straighten the front knee—just a bit—and...

35. ...strike the ball with the clubhead, staying...

36. ...relaxed, and...

37. ...keeping the clubhead flush to the ball, with...

38. ...your head still down.

39. Swing through the ball, as you...

40. ...keep your head down, and...

41. ...rotate your shoulders forward, and...

42. ...rotate your hips forward, while...

43. ...uncocking your wrists, then...

44. ...begin the follow through.

45. Stay parallel to the ball and target.

46. Roll your wrists through the shot.

47. Bend your front elbow, and...

48. ...follow with your back arm straightish.

49. Keep your head down!

50. Ask someone where the ball went.

Section II

Equipment

6 Top Golf Club Manufacturers

Clubs are very personal things. But they represent a major problem. Mainly, you need to have them. After all, how often have you felt that you'd be better off if you could just heave and/or kick the ball? Sorry. Using one of these odd sticks is required. There are a lot of club makers out there, many of whom can create custom clubs just for you. But this list features the best of the mass-market manufacturers.

1. Callaway Golf

When Ely Callaway started the company in 1982, he called it Callaway Hickory Stick USA, Inc. Why? Because he made hickory-shafted putters and wedges. But in 1986, the company created irons they called S2H2, for "Short, Straight, Hollow Hosel. That not only created a market sensation, it required that the company change its name.

In the 1990s, the club maker blasted itself into market leadership with the Big Bertha. Named after a World War I cannon, oversized Big Bertha Woods did for golf clubs what the oversized racket did for tennis: They gave us all the illusion that we were better than we actually are. By the mid-90s, along came Big Bertha Irons, the Great Big Bertha Titanium Fairway Wood, and Big Bertha Gold Irons, all conceived to inflate our damaged egos. It was just that ability to make us duffers feel better about ourselves that qualifies this company to be among the top five in this list.

2. Taylor Made

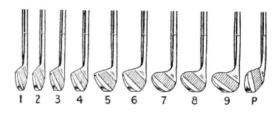

Taylor Made has only been making clubs since 1979, but it's been at the head of the pack for most of that time. The company's forte—as most leading club makers claim—is its commitment to technological innovation, and it has been a leader in the development of, among other things, metal woods. (Having the power and size of the Adidas-Salomon Group, the second-largest sporting goods company in the world, behind the company doesn't hurt its ability to make its presence felt, however.) Indeed it was a Taylor Made metal wood that was the first of its kind to win the Masters in 1994, and it's now the number-one driver on both the PGA Tour and the European PGA Tour. Taylor Made's Burner Bubble Oversize Irons were an industry sales leader during the 1996-1998 period. Its latest innovation is something called the InerGel golf ball, which no doubt makes Taylor Made's clubs seem better, although neither the clubs nor the gelatin-centered ball have straightened out my shots.

3. Ping

How can you argue with a name like this? More importantly, how radical was it to start by making just one, specialized club? It was Karsten Solheim's reinvention of the putter that put this company on the map.

Working as an engineer for General Electric, Karsten puttered with his putter for quite a while; then in 1959, he figured he had something marketable. Why call it *Ping*? Purportedly because of the musical sound it made when it contacted the ball. He began making and selling these things out of his garage. He continued to develop putters. By the end of 1965, he had created 21 models. In 1966, he added the Anser putter (so called because "The Answer" was too long to engrave on the head), and by 1967 he quit his day job and began making a full line of clubs. He innovated irons with perimeter weighting, heel-toe balance, and an offset hosel. The rest, as they say, is history.

4. Cleveland

Here's another guy—Roger Cleveland to be exact—who started out in a boutique club-making operation. Back in 1979, he set out to meticulously re-create replicas of classic golf clubs from the 1940s and 1950s. Today, the company produces the number-one wedge used on the PGA, Nike, and LPGA Tours. Recent company growth can be credited to the French ski-maker Rossignol, which acquired the company in 1990, and it has been expanding and improving the product ever since.

5. Orlimar

Yet one more company that started small, Orlimar was founded by Lou Ortiz, who began with a club repair business in the basement of a converted stable in San Francisco. His first clubs were handcrafted persimmon drivers and then fairway woods. Their secret? Tender loving care and the best persimmon wood that money could buy. Now, Orlimar is considered one of the hottest golf companies in America. The Ortiz family remains active in day-to-day company operations, even though they're turning out some 10,000 clubs a day. When Callaway Golf put Big Bertha on the course, Orlimar was forced to abandon wooden clubs; it began to work metal woods in 1995. Orlimar's latest effort is an iron constructed from a unique iron alloy with a high chromium and copper content. (It's getting so you have to be a metallurgist to understand these clubs.) Sales in 1999 reached $80 million.

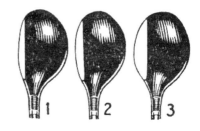

6. Mizuno

Mizuno rests its reputation on its irons. It claims that they are the number-one irons on both the European and U.S. PGA Tours. These guys are not Johnny-come-latelies; the company has been in the sporting goods business since 1906, and it can now lay claim to being the world's largest general sporting goods manufacturer, offering more than 30,000 different products worldwide. Mizuno marketed the first all-titanium iron (the MGC-35) in 1989 and the first all-titanium wood in the world (the Ti-110) in 1990. Size, innovation, high regard from the pros: That is why Mizuno makes this list.

6 Historically Remarkable Golf Clubs

You'll notice that two of the clubs on the following list are putters. Truth is, putting incites more remarkable—if not downright bizarre—club designs than any other stroke. And, yet, it seems so easy!

1. The Schenectady Putter

This putter earned its nickname because it was invented circa 1901 by Arthur F. "Frank" Knight, an engineer at the Schenectady, New York, General Electric plant. Walter Travis tied for second in the 1902 U.S. Open using this club; he won the 1903 U.S. Amateur Championship with it, sparking enormous sales and copycat clubs from major manufacturers, MacGregor and Spalding among them. Even back then, success in majors was a club maker's best advertising. The club's secret? A center shaft. Alas, The Royal and Ancient Golf Club Committee on the Rules of Golf declared it, among other center-shafted clubs, illegal. The USGA, however, did not. It wasn't until 1959 that the Royal and Ancient Golf Club finally lifted its ban on center-shafted clubs.

2. Fairlie Irons and Smith Irons

Mr. Francis Archibald Fairlie was a noted amateur golfer who learned the game from the famous Brit, Old Tom Morris. In the early 1890s, in order to accommodate his new swing—which he changed from a large, roundhouse style to a compact backswing—he designed his own irons, for which he was granted

Patent 6681 in 1891. Fairlie always had problems with shanking shots (don't we all?), so he moved the blade in front of the hosel, effectively eliminating the problem (for himself, at least). The term "Fairlie iron" was commonly used for at least 25 years.

Smith-style irons, which appeared three years after the Fairlie iron, also addressed the shanking problem. Patented by G.F. Smith, a London-area amateur golfer, these irons kept the club face in line with the shaft, but the hosel was bowed like a gooseneck behind the blade. In addition, Smith provided blade stability at impact by perimeter weighting the back of the club head. Smith irons not only had weighted heels and toes, they were designed with a concave back. Perimeter weighting? Concave back? Sound familiar? The Smiths were very popular; they were, perhaps, the Pings of their day.

3. The Sand Wedge

Walter Hagen was famous for his short game, particularly his bunker play. Although his career took place before the actual invention of the sand wedge as an individual club, he created something he called a "sand iron" which featured an extended flange and a concave face. That extended flange remains universal in one form or another today. The modern sand wedge is attributed to Gene Sarazen circa 1932, who added some lead to the front edge of an iron, allowing him to ride the club head through the sand instead of digging into it. The club was instrumental in helping him win the British and U.S. Opens in 1932.

4. The Taylor Made Metal Wood

Modernists would say that Taylor Made introduced the first metal woods in 1979. But the first successfully marketed metal woods came from Reginald Thomas Brougham, a London toy manufacturer, in 1893. Still, it was the Taylor Made version that stuck and revolutionized the game, relegating wooden woods to garages, attics, and collectors' caches everywhere.

5. Big Bertha

Well, it had happened to tennis rackets, so you could bet it was going to happen to golf clubs: oversizing; increased sweet spot; forgiveness for the sin of off-centered whacks. The Callaway Golf Company, of course, introduced its groundbreaking Big Bertha in 1991 and revolutionized everything. Here was a golf club that actually helped golfers obtain straighter shots on off-center hits. And it probably allowed them to hit on-center hits farther. Sales that skyrocketed into the stratosphere tell the rest of the story.

6. Ping Putter

And here's that other putter, the club that vaulted Solheim Karsten from his garage into an international business. Clearly he was on to something more than just a gimmick. Karsten's design aimed at creating a head that would reduce the tendency of the ball to skip and bounce. He achieved this by attaching the shaft directly to the sole plate instead of to the shaft at the top. He called it "torsion sole" construction. The head itself was hollow, looking, as one reviewer wrote, "from the top somewhat like a dugout canoe with square ends." The result was a bit of give upon impact that produced a rebounding effect. A golfer had to shorten his stroke some, but the resulting over-spin minimized bouncing, and guiding the ball became easier. The price in 1959 for this highly popular, high specialized weapon? $17.50 each.

The Best Golf Club Names of All Time

"What's in a name?" Shakespeare once queried. It depends on your perspective. Although there's something methodical and pragmatic in numbering golf clubs relative to their loft, there's certainly a lack of romance, or just plain imagination. Which term stirs something in your soul: 2-wood or Brassie? 4-iron or Mid-Mashie? It's no wonder club makers have taken to thinking up techno-romantic names for their club lines. The clubs themselves are so dull. Here, then, a tribute to the best club names from a time when the rough was *really* rough, lost golf balls could cost you a week's wages, and clubs were fashioned from trees and branches, not forges.

1. Spoon

Golfers like this. It conjures an image of trying to feed the ball to the hole. It also reminds us of the kind of implement we'd like to have when our ball is (as it so often is) buried in a sand trap. Plus, there's a romantic connotation of that old-fashioned term for making-out—spooning. Today the equivalent club is a 3-wood.

2. Niblick

Whatever that means. It sounds like a baby's toy. Which is perhaps what a 9-iron, the modern niblick, really is. Which is maybe why it's the only iron some of us can use effectively. Gotta get it up in the air? Hand us the 9-iron. Lying 300 yards straight out with water at 75 yards? 9-iron, please. We'll nibble our way to the green. Niblick? Nibble? Get it? No matter, it doesn't help our game.

3. Mashie

Now a mashie is a 5-iron, a club most golfers seldom, if ever, actually used. But it does describe what happens to any ball we can manage to keep in play for more than three holes. Mashed.

4. Spade Mashie

Another infrequently used club, equal to a 6-iron, but clearly a useful club because it sounds like it doubles as a gardening tool.

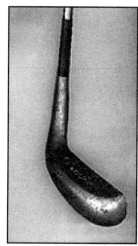

A Mashie

5. Cleek

This club makes the list because it rhymes with geek, which is what many of us feel like when we try to hit golf balls, and with creek, which is where many of our lost balls can be found. Today, a cleek is a 4-wood, which is another club most golfers never actually use.

A Cleek

5 Historically Significant Golf Balls

Today there's a lot of hype devoted to golf balls. They can fly straighter, higher, longer, or better, all the while eliciting better feel, control, or touch. They come constructed with gel centers and titanium covers, and pro golfers endorse them to assure us of success. Of course, there isn't any golf ball that's going anywhere farther or straighter if you line yourself up wrong and swing with an open club face. Perhaps someone should patent a golf ball that's guaranteed to slice.

Anyway, once upon a time, golf balls were stuffed with feathers and built by hand by true craftsmen. Then, rubber came into it, and the sport has never been the same.

1. The Gutta Percha

The gutta percha ball created a radical change in the game when it replaced the "feathery," those handmade leather balls stuffed with feathers. Gutta percha is a sap-like substance secreted by trees that can be molded when heated to 212 degrees Fahrenheit. It will hold its shape when cooled.

"Gutties" could be produced much more easily than featheries, lasted longer, and therefore were less expensive and became immediately more popular.

2. The Dimpled Gutta Percha

For quite a while, skilled golfers had noticed that scuffed gutties—those that had been hit a few times or slightly cut—flew better and more true. In 1880, someone put a gutty in a mold and—voila!—dimples. Golf balls have had dimples ever since.

3. The Haskell Ball

In 1898, Coburn Haskell created the first rubber-cored ball. Perhaps the only comparable change in a major sport would be the difference between baseballs of the so-called "dead ball" era and their modern counterparts. Haskell worked with

Early rubber-cored balls. (left scored, right dimpled)

one Bertram Work, who in turn worked for the B.F. Goodrich Company, to develop a construction of rubber thread wound around a solid rubber core. These balls flew at least 25 yards farther off the tee, but early versions were deemed *too* lively and hard to putt. When Spalding developed the balata cover, made from the gum of the bully tree, and created an aerodynamically superior dimple pattern for it in 1908, the rubber-core ball became a fixture.

4. The Pneu-matic

Unable to let good enough alone, the B.F. Goodrich folks brought to market in 1906 a golf ball with a rubber core filled with compressed air called the "Pneu-matic." Yes, it went a long way. Unfortunately, it showed a tendency to explode in warm weather, sometimes right in a golfer's pocket. Can you imagine the lawsuits that would generate today?

5. The Top-Flite

Spalding introduced the Top-Flite in 1972. It was the first two-piece ball. Today, the Top-Flite XL family of golf balls is played by more people worldwide than any other golf ball, including nearly 25 percent of all U.S. golfers.

5 Top Golf Shoes for Today

I t's sad but true. Anything that you do on your feet—running, walking, skiing, thinking—requires good shoes. Especially as you get older. It doesn't matter what kind of foot you're stuck with. High arches, flat feet, hammer toes, or feet with your brains in them: No matter, you want them to be comfortable. So shoes matter, because even if you intend to ride a first-class limo around the course, you still have to stand up to hit the ball, and jammed toes, blisters, or aching arches will prevent you not only from doing it right, but from enjoying yourself.

Which features are important? Waterproofing is good, especially if you play early in the morning when the dew is still on the grass, or when unexpected downpours get you, or when you decide to wade in the water to retrieve your expensive golf ball.

Soft spikes, too, are recommended, if for no other reason than more and more courses are restricting you to their use. Besides, they're better for course maintenance, which makes them better for the environment, and that's better for all of us. Logic says you should use shoes that afford you replaceable spikes, but nobody says you need to be logical. If you own Nike stock, or some other major shoe company's stock, you might want to go with footwear that demands total shoe replacement when the spikes wear down, just to keep company sales up. Your choice.

But, it's fit that counts most. No matter what the price or manufacturer's reputation, it's how the shoes fit *your* feet that counts. Our list contains the best or most popular brands, but none of this may apply to you. If the shoe fits, wear it.

1. FootJoy

Typically recommended: DryJoys. FootJoy makes a lot of golf shoes. You'll maybe pay $130 for these, for which you get something called ICT (Interactive Comfort Technology); "Fit-Beds" with some kind of gel that is supposed to absorb heat when it's hot and release heat when it's cold; greens-friendly soft spikes; and, most of all, a two-year limited waterproof warranty. The manufacturer has adapted fancy names for "torque control" and other performance-related stuff, which it must think sells shoes.

To find out where to buy these shoes, or which other models the company offers, contact FootJoy, 333 Bridge Street, Fairhaven, MA 02719; Web site: *www.footjoy.com*; Phone: 800-225-8500.

2. Etonic

Typically recommended: Stabilites. For a mere $70, you can get traditional spikes or soft ones and something called "traction stabilizer technology for enhanced stability." Because these are less expensive, their waterproof guarantee only lasts a year. To get more information, contact Etonic, 147 Centre Street, Brockton, MA 02402; Web site: *www.etonic.com*; Phone: 800-638-6642.

3. Nike

Typically recommended: Air Max Press. The Microsoft of sports footwear, Nike has taken all its running/basketball/tennis/and so on experience and decided to make golf shoes based on athletic shoe technology. The result is a kind of tennis shoe for the links with waterproofing, stiff support yet comfortable soles, and about an $80 price tag. Look out for non-replaceable cleats, however. Nike shoes are sold all over the place, but to pin down a local dealer contact Nike Golf, One Bowerman Drive, Beaverton OR 97005; Web site: *www.nikegolfclub.com*; Phone: 800-806-6453.

4. Reebok

Typically recommended: DMX Trac. For about $110 you get some bars installed into the interior of the shoe that will keep you laterally stable. (As opposed to vertically stable?) And some medial nubs allow you to roll easily into the backswing. Then, Reebok adds a layer of customized moving air. (Just exactly *how* do you customize moving air?) Anyway, you get the picture; for more information, contact Reebok International Ltd., PO Box 1060, Ronks, PA 17573; Web site: *www.reebok.com*; Phone: 800-833-6331.

5. Walter Genuin

Okay, these guys are the Rolls Royce of golf shoes. If you can afford to plunk down $350, you should try these babies on. You'll get calfskin leather outsoles, Gortex waterproofing, and status beyond your wildest dreams. To find out more, contact Walter Genuin, 6703 Levellan Drive, Suite A, Dallas, TX 75252; Web site: *www.waltergenuin.com*; Phone: 800-531-2218.

11

5 Top Golf Bags for Today

What's in a bag? Good question. You might find just about anything in there, which is why buying a bag is such a personal decision. Some folks just need room for their clubs and a pocket for some balls, tees, and a glove. Some need to carry the entire house in there: cell phone, ice and drinks, Palm Pilot, electronic range finder, a favorite book, golf instructional tips, a rain parka, extra shoe spikes, a change of clothes, maybe even the Manhattan phone book. So, knowing what you need in a bag is an experiential matter. You go out there, play rounds until you're comfortable, until you get a sense of what you must have out there with you. Do you walk the course? Do you ride an imitation Rolls Royce cart? Do you want to physically lug the bag around, or will you drag it on wheels? All these factors come into play, with three things emerging as most important: weight, especially if you're going to carry it; size/number of pockets, to accommodate whatever junk must travel the course with you; and club storage, which includes easily organizing your clubs and padding of some kind to protect them.

Like all categories of equipment for major participation sports, the number of choices here borders on the criminal. In truth, the world could get by just fine with two or three models of bags from two or three makers. But, alas, dozens are out there from among which to choose. Here are five we like. Why just *five* out of a million? Why not 10 or 20? Because five is enough to satisfy any addict. Or it should be.

1. Sun Mountain

Example: Summit. For something on the order of $170, you get a bag that manages to combine goodly size with reasonable weight. Toss in a sturdy stand mechanism, a ton of pockets, full-length padded dividers, and a removable valuables pouch (which can double as a purse?), and you're onto something. Oh yeah, the straps are nicely padded and the thing holds a full load of goods. Good.

You can get information on the whole Sun Mountain line or locate a dealer by visiting *www.sunmountain.com*, calling 800-227-9224, or writing Sun Mountain, Golf Bags and Tech Divisions, P.O. Box 7727, 301 N First Street, Missoula, MT 59802.

2. Callaway

Example: Callaway Golf Daytripper Stand Bags or Callaway Golf Mini Tour Staff carrying bag. I like the look of the Callaway bags. That's good enough for me.  The features are all there, the price also runs about $170, but with the Callaway logo, the bags look cool and professional, even if you're playing Spalding beginner clubs.

Need to know more? Visit *www.callawaygolf.com*, call 800-228-2767, or write Callaway Golf Company, 2285 Rutherford Road, Carlsbad, CA 92008.

3. Izzo

Example: Delight 300. Another $170 item. A very cool thing here is that not only is the bag pretty light, but folks who don't want or need to carry a lot of trinkets can make it even lighter by detaching the main pocket. It has a sturdy stand, is comfortable to carry, and *will* store the kitchen sink if you keep that pocket in place. You can also add dual straps.

We also like that Izzo makes the Delight 300 in a lefty model and the Izzo Delight for Her 300. Such thoughtful folks!

To find out more, visit *www.izzo.com*; call 800-284-1220; or write IZZO Systems, LLC, 1635 Commons Parkway, Macedon, NY 14502.

4. Bennington

Example: Camel Lite Stand Bag. Camels rank among the world's best schlepping animals, but you can't get one for just $100. And even if you could, you couldn't take it to the golf course with you to carry your clubs. So, why not get a bag that turns you into a camel-like schlepper? This has a dual strap carry system, an "E-Z" grip handle, and it can be equipped with a so-called lumbar caddy for around-the-waist support so you'll not get an aching back while humping a round with it.

To find a retailer or get more information, visit *www.benningtongolf.com*; call 800-624-2580; or write to Bennington Golf, 2500 White Road, Irvine, CA 92714.

5. Lynx

Example: Staff. Here's one from the upscale department. For $300 to $400, you can get a very sturdy, very lightweight stand bag with fully five major pockets and a large five-point harness sling. We'll slap five to that!

You can learn more at *www.lynxgolf.com*, by calling 800-233-5969, or by writing Lynx Customer Service, 11000 North IH-35, Austin, TX 78753.

12 10 Amusing (and Questionably Effective) Golf Gadgets...

and 8 Gadgets That Just Might Prove Worthwhile

Few sports inspire the number of training and ease-of-play devices that golf does, from handicap calculators to scopes for scoping out the lay of the land, to elaborate contraptions that require an acre of backyard in which to set up, to really draconian swing-improvement contrivances that look like something from a medieval torture chamber.

Why? What causes people to not only invent these things, but to actually buy them? We refer you back to Chapter 5 and the elements of the golf swing. Clearly, anything that's so fundamental to the game and successfully performing at it, while being simultaneously so complex, will unavoidably engender arcane and sometimes wonderfully silly contraptions conceived to mysteriously deliver magical results.

All of the contrivances presented here were found for sale at one of my favorite Web sites: *www.findgolfstuff.com.* Go ahead, look them up!

10 Amusing (and Questionably Effective) Golf Gadgets

1. Carpenter's Mirror

This is a rectangular acrylic mirror that you lay at your own feet. It's designed to let you properly align your head and foot positions while addressing the ball, and also line yourself up for swing positions. This happens to be something most golfers desperately need; no matter how improbable it may seem, I cannot ever tell when I'm properly lined up and aiming the shot in the correct direction. This thing promises to assist in checking out foot and shoulder alignment, hand position, and the club shaft positioning at nine o'clock and top of the swing, all the while monitoring head movement. But, because it's all

done with mirrors, it's all perceived upside down and/or reversed, is it not? I fear that looking at things upside down and backwards will yield only further confusion. Cost: $49.95.

2. Figure 8 Strap

Well, strap me down and slap me silly. Here's an elastic strap, shaped like a figure eight, that purports to "work your hands, arms, and shoulders together!" In other words, tie yourself up by the arms above the elbows and you get a connected, torso-controlled swing. By keeping the elbows together, the strap purports to not only develop proper sequential motion, but to prevent over-swinging. It can be used at home for "shadow" swinging practice. Price: $16.95.

3. Flammer

Here's a gizmo that promises to make you swing like Iron Byron, the flawless swing machine used at ball-testing facilities. Just attach this device to your sternum using the clip-on harness. An adjustable rod extends and attaches to the club at the top of the grip, and controls your swing pattern, eliminating wrist over-cocking and over-pronation or supination. All this for a mere $99.95? A bargain at twice the price!

4. Golfsmith Putting Track

An aluminum track with parallel, calibrated rails that monitors your putter's face position throughout your stroke. It's like having your own school hall monitor for your putter, who will automatically tattle when bad things are happening. Price: $39.95.

5. Groove Tube Full Circle Trainer

This is one of those draconian devices mentioned earlier. It is a huge tube that provides guidance for your swing's plane. Just make sure you're riding the rails from the 9 o'clock to 3 o'clock positions, and you'll soon be "just doing it." Perhaps they should provide a subway track third rail that shocks you when you get out of line, or a parachute for when you drop out of the plane? Cost: $129.95.

6. Heavy Hitter Driver

Two, two, two devices in one — from Gary Player himself! A precision-balanced club with a perimeter-weighted club head, matched to a weighted shaft, which develops all the muscles required for swinging (the golf club that is, not spouse swapping or anything like that), and a molded grip to make sure you're keeping the proper grip on things. This comes in three models to fit your needs perfectly, and it works much  better than putting a baseball bat donut on your driver. For you, just: $99.95.

7. Impact Bag with Instructional Video

Here's something we all need. A punching bag for our golf clubs. Even if you don't develop perfect power and a solid, assertive impact, as the designers claim you will, you can certainly vent your frustrations and take out your aggressions on this thing. Whammo! Take that, you old bag! The Impact Bag comes with a special slice-cure supplement, guaranteed to cure your slice in 60 seconds, they say. Maybe we should try a vitamin supplement, too? Price: $39.95, with video.

8. John Daly Power Groove

More muscle memory development, here at twice the price (a mere $200). But, hey, if John Daly says it works, who are we to argue? You rig up a "Gyro coupler" (uh-huh) to the club grip, use the "sight alignment convex mirror attached to the base" to line up your swing and - voila! - swing low sweet chariot and take that ball right on home. "It's that easy!" says the ad copy. Easy? Gyro gizmos and alignment mirrors? Doesn't sound all that easy to me. But, heck, it must be easier than rocket science. You can have it for just $199.95.

9. Platform Swing Trainer

You can use this device anywhere there's room to swing a club. It'll tell you if you're a hooker, slicer, dicer, or straight-shooter (as if you didn't already know). It kind of looks like a miniature, horizontal baseball set, but with a golf ball that's on a heavy-duty wire. When you hit it, you can tell which way the ball would have gone by how it goes around in a circle, if you don't get dizzy first. Selling price is a mere $31.95.

10. Tac-Tic Elbow

I thought this had something to do with breath mints! Not so. It's a device that looks like an elbow brace, but it makes an audible noise—not dissimilar to the sound of tendinitis or tennis elbow at work—when the elbow does something wrong. Put it on your lead arm, and you'll hear about any break down in the elbow from the clicking noise. Put it on your following arm, and it clicks at you when the elbow reaches a right angle, which *should* be at the top of the backswing. Hear it too soon, and you're being bad. Price: $39.95.

...And 8 Gadgets That Just Might Prove Worthwhile

1. Formed Grips

Is there anything more basic than holding the club? Probably not. After all, hold it wrong and you'll hit it wrong. So, why not try a grip that guides your hands exactly to where they should be? Great idea. It allows you to hold the club right the first time and accustoms you to the proper feel. A truly worthwhile training item for less than $10.

2. Steve LaPorte Putting Green

There are a surprising number of at-home or in-the-office practice putting devices out there. This one, if you can afford it, seems one of the best. It's pretty simple to use and set up, and it recreates realistic putting pretty well. The manufacturer claims it will also enhance your home's interior decoration, but that's a stretch. If you can spend more than $1,000, you can get one that measures a full 5' x 11' and includes a pin with flag and pads for adjustable breaks. Too much money? The 4' x 9' version sells for less than $500. Still too much? Try the 20" x 9' for about $250. All of these, by the way, come with carrying cases, just in case you want to take them on the road and pretend you're on your own PGA tour.

3. Bickler Putting Aide

The manufacturer claims the pros use these to maintain a proper angle between the forearm and the putter shaft. It's an inexpensive device that attaches to the top of your grip. It makes you keep the club face square at impact and prevents wrist breakdown. Hey, for $20, what can you lose?

4. Birdiemaster

More portable putting mastery. This gizmo utilizes a graduated series of rings to provide smaller and smaller targets that make putts progressively more difficult. Soon, the maker assures us, we'll be deadly accurate! Which is better than being dead. Cost: $16.95.

5. Pin Balls

Still having trouble striking your putts on the square even after you've tried the Bickler device noted above? Try these Siamese twin balls. They're joined together so they'll only roll straight when stuck perfectly on center. They'll also look good sitting on your bookshelf, and they only cost $15 or so.

6. Short Flyte Balls

More in-home fun. You can whack these babies as hard as you like and they won't go more than 30 yards. Much better than slamming your fist against the wall when you're angry; even if you don't improve your game, you can take out your frustrations on them. The maker claims that, unlike other plastic practice balls, these hide a hard center core that gives a realistic feel when you whack 'em, but they have a foam cover that protects your Ming vases and other decorative valuables. You can get four of these gentle babies for about $10.

7. Auto Golf Net

Okay, golfers can't always get out to the links or the driving range, but they know they need to practice and they certainly don't have the square acreage in the backyard to hit away. What golfers need is a practice net that will let them go full bore but not break windows down the block. A surprising number of folks make these nets, but this version is among the best. It's a pop-up job, and to use it, you need a minuscule 11 square yards of space. It's portable, so you can take it on visits to the in-laws and give yourself something to do. No hitting wedges into this thing, however—unless you stand practically *inside* it—and then, who knows, the ball might come back to whack you. But, drastic slices or hooks are safely caught by it. The cost? About $170—less than a new driver.

8. CaddyRack

I don't know about you, but I am inherently slobbish and have been known to hunt around in my golf bags for untold minutes looking for my seven-iron (especially when I've managed to leave it on the ground three holes back). This little item puts an end to all that in-bag clutter. It'll organize and protect your irons by supporting the heads in a separate compartment and keeping the shafts apart. You just need a bag with parallel dividers, a strong desire to end your slovenly ways, and $38.

Section III

Publications

15 Great Golf Books that Deserve to be Read

For writers, there's never a need to be admonished to read. Nor is there ever a need for an excuse to sit down with a good book. For writers who golf — well, the conclusion is obvious. While you might not be a writer, you *are* a golfer (why else would you be reading this silly tome?). So read the following, starting immediately.

1. *The Inner Game of Golf*, by W. Timothy Gallwey (Random House, 1979; Revised edition, 1998)

The entire realm of sports psychology blasted off with this series of inner game books, and this one remains a must-read. A million readers can't be wrong, can they?

2. *Bob Hope's Confessions of a Hooker*, by Bob Hope (Doubleday, 1985)

Okay, maybe you have to be a certain age to fully appreciate Bob Hope. I certainly hope not. Bob Hope was to golf what Jack Benny was to the violin, and this remains a comic classic, with anecdotes and pearls of wisdom and plenty of celebrity appearances, including Arnold Palmer, Jack Nicklaus, Bing Crosby, John F. Kennedy, and Jackie Gleason.

3. *The Illustrated History of Golf*, by Allan Elliott and John Allan May (Gallery Books, 1990)

We should all know our heritage and where we come from. Here's a tome that tells us. Sure, you'll feel bad knowing that guys like Young Tom Morris could play the St. Andrews Old Course better than you'll ever do using homemade clubs and a feathery ball, but it's every golfer's heritage! Treasure it.

4. *Down Hill Lies and Other Falsehoods*, by Rex Lardner (Hawthorn Books, 1973)

More much-needed humor by a classic humorist.

5. *How to Live with a Golfaholic*, by Mark Oman (A Golfaholics Anonymous Book, 1986)

And still more much-needed humor. Give a copy to your non-playing spouse, children, mother-in-law, and psychiatrist. They'll thank you for it.

6. *The Complete Book of Golf*: *A N.Y. Times Scrapbook History* (N.Y. Times Publishing, 1980)

This book features more history, with plenty of photos, from "the paper of record." What could be more authoritative than that?

7. *The Bogey Man*, by George Plimpton (Harper and Row, 1968)

Plimpton has been poking his nose onto other people's playing fields for a long, long time. His perspective, insight, and humor do not fade from relevance and revelation.

8. *The Best of Wodehouse on Golf*, by P.G. Wodehouse, D.R. Bensen, editor (Houghton Mifflin, 1999)

The master humorist takes on the game he loved. Bless him.

9. *Buried Lies (True Tales And Tall Stories)*, by Peter Jacobson with Jack Sheehan (Penguin USA, 1994)

Now here's a classic that all golfers can immerse themselves in. After all, only fishermen weave taller tales than golfers.

10. *500 Years of Golf Balls*, by John F. Hotchkiss (Antique Trader, 1997)

All right, this might be a bit esoteric. But it's fascinating.

11. *A Good Walk Spoiled: Days and Nights on the PGA Tour*, by John Feinstein (Little, Brown, 1996)

This is a classic by a superb writer who somehow manages to humanize the PGA masters of the game, especially the guys struggling to hold on, make the cut, and stay alive on the tour. Feinstein shows us just how incredibly difficult this game is. As if we didn't already know!

12. *Harvey Penick's Little Red Book: Lessons and Teachings from a Lifetime in Golf*, by Harvey Penick, with Bud Shrake (Simon and Schuster, 1992)

This is the original volume of thoughts on playing the game by the sport's greatest teacher. A must for anyone who hacks.

13. *"And Then Jack Said to Arnie..." A Collection of the Greatest True Golf Stories of All Time*, by Don Wade, with Lee Trevino (NTC/Contemporary Publishing, 1992)

The first book in what has now become a series. Good gossip always makes for juicy reading; good gossip written well makes for a good time.

14. *Blue Fairways: A Route 1 Golf Odyssey*, by Charles Slack (Henry Holt, 2000)

This recent book is a marvelous travelogue.

15. *Fairways to Heaven: The Journeyman's Guide to the Best of American Golf,* by Trent Ricker and Michael Stevens (Pin High Publishing, 1997)

Here is a pair of guys who drove 27,000 miles, played 90 public courses, and lost only 283 balls. You have to at least admire their fortitude and tenacity. They cover 56 courses in detail, and maintain a purist's eye, a critic's "show me" attitude, and a nice sense of humor. You even get hole diagrams, course information, and scorecards.

10 Worthwhile Golf Instruction Books

Golfers never cease analyzing, obsessing, and dreaming about their game. Now, whether one can actually learn to play better by reading a book is debatable. But clearly, millions of Nicklaus wanna-be's do think so, because hundreds of how-to golf books line the shelves of bookstores and libraries everywhere. Here's a list of books that, if they don't bring your game down to par, will at least provide plenty of food for thought.

1. *Harvey Penick's Little Red Book: Lessons and Teachings From a Lifetime in Golf,* by Harvey Penick with Bud Shrake (Simon and Schuster, 1992)

The first of the Penick books, it is still probably the best book out there. Period. It's golf; it's life; relax, man, and go for it.

2. *Golf Is a Woman's Game,* by Jane Horn (Adams Media Corporation, 1997)

Despite its title, the author claims the book is worthwhile for males as well as females. Well, she's right. More than 40 myths women have been taught about their golf swings are covered here, with instruction on how women can "just do it" the right way. Nearly all of which applies to male types, too.

3. *Naked on the First Tee: An Essential Guide for New Women Golfers*, by Ann Kelly (GA Kelly Publishing, 1999)

Guys, give this book to your significant other if you're interested in getting her started on the course. It addresses all the fundamental "dumb" questions everyone's always afraid to ask. And you know what? Beginner males will benefit, too. Not much on technique or instruction, but a wealth of golf culture. And we all want to be cultured, don't we?

4. *Putt Like the Pros: Dave Pelz's Scientific Way to Improving Your Stroke, Reading Greens, and Lowering Your Score*, by Dave Pelz and Nick Mastroni (HarperCollins, 1991)

Pelz is in the process of putting out a series of instruction books that cover the entire game. He's the acknowledged master, so why not listen to him? If it's *actually* possible to improve your play from reading, his books are the ones to read. Of course, you'll still have to actually go out and practice and play, but if you're on an airplane or something, you can be reading this stuff and improving as you go.

5. *Dave Pelz's Short Game Bible: Master the Finesse Swing and Lower Your Score*, by Dave Pelz with James A. Frank and Lee Janzen (Broadway Books, 1999)

See #4 on this list.

6. *Ben Hogan's Five Lessons: The Modern Fundamentals of Golf*, by Ben Hogan (Simon and Schuster, 1989)

Hogan originally wrote this book in 1957, and it is amazing how much still holds true. It's a classic. Even though they didn't have oversized clubs and fancy alloys back in those days, swing fundamentals haven't changed. Check out the drawings.

7. *Golf for Lefties*, by Bill Burr (Masters Press, 1997)

Lefties *are* different. Why shouldn't they have their own book?

8. *Classic Golf Tips*, by Tommy Armour (NTC Publishing Group, 1995)

Here's a guy who coached the likes of Babe Didrikson Zaharias and Julius Boros. An avid golfing friend of mine values this as the best in her extensive library.

9. *Golf Is Not a Game of Perfect*, by Bob J. Rotella with Bob Cullen (Simon and Schuster Trade, 1995).

Oh how 1990s this is! Rotella is known as a "performance consultant," and he focuses on attitude and mind-set. Well, if the guy insists that the primary issues are to focus on fun and love the challenge, I can't find fault with that. Writers have the same problem when facing a blank page.

10. *Golf Magazine's Complete Book of Golf Instruction*, by James A. Frank, Lorin Anderson, and John Andrisani (Golf Magazine/Harry N. Abrams, 1997)

Here's a serious book for serious players. Possibly too serious, frankly, but for folks who read publications like *Golf*, it brings together the best of the magazine's instruction articles. Read it before you go to bed at night; then you'll dream of perfect shots.

12 Golf Magazines Worth Their Subscription Prices

This list makes no comment on these magazines. Next time you're in a bookstore (to buy a copy of this book as a present for a friend, associate, or loved one, no doubt), buy copies of these magazines. Read them all and either you'll gain an incredibly diverse and well-rounded perspective on the game and all its aspects, or you'll never stop reading and no one else will be able to use the bathroom you're occupying.

1. *Golf*
2. *Golf Digest*
3. *Golf Travel*
4. *Links*
5. *Today's Golfer*
6. *Maximum Golf*
7. *Bunkered*
8. *Golf for Women*
9. *Golf Illustrated*
10. *Golf Week*
11. *Schwing*
12. *Golf World*

16

10 Worthwhile Online Golf Magazines

Given the nature of the Net, one can only hope that these online magazines are still there when you go looking for them.

1. *Golfonline.com*

This is the online version of *Golf Magazine*, done in conjunction with ESPN. It has all the requisite information, from celebrity profiles and instruction to tournament results, travel, and course rating. Lacks humor, however. But then again, so do so many serious golfers.

2. *Golf Illustrated (www.golfillustrated.com)*

The online version of the serious golfer's weekly magazine. For some reason, it also gives news from CNBC.com and stock market news from CBS. Do all golfers worry about their portfolios while calculating their handicaps?

3. *Golf Digest Online (www.golfdigest.com)*

This online site for the major magazine is good for those who don't want to pay to subscribe to the print edition. It offers more information and features than most onlines will give you for free.

4. *The Sporting News Golf* (*www.sportingnews.com/golf*)

This is the site for the hard-core competitive sports nut who wants articles on the tour and its players, plus all the inside dope on the major sports leagues and betting lines.

5. *Ladies Golf Journal* (*www.iglou.com/lgjonline*)

This all-inclusive magazine presents features, interviews, a BBS, and a no-nonsense approach. The magazine is very likeable and has real personality.

6. *The 19th Hole* (*19thhole.com*)

Here is a little bit of this and a little bit of that, all very thorough, however, and constantly updated. And, oh boy, the links!

7. *Greenside Journal of Golf* (*www.golfball.com/green/greenmag.htm*)

An affiliate of *Golfballs.com* and *The Virtual Golfer*, this is a good general interest site that reads like a magazine because—surprise!—it *is* a magazine. And one that's not too commercially oriented, either, so they can offer odd insights (how a golf ball really works), as well as travel, course design, and criticism, and other forms of golf wisdom.

8. *Divot.com*

This site bills itself as a "literary magazine for golfers" that offers fiction and opinion. It's really an outlet for editor R.N.A. Smith with a bunch of well-known (John Updike, for example) and not so well-known contributors. The site considers itself, also, to be a "public club" allowing anyone to submit golf fiction or opinion pieces. It's a bit full of itself, but it's actually good reading, which in itself is unusual for the Web.

9. *Badgolfmonthly.com*

"The site for the golfer who really sucks," it says of itself. I can relate. I like the "Hall of Shame" section.

10. *joeditzel.com*

Before I came upon this site, I didn't know Joe Ditzel from a hole in the wall. Or a hole in one, for that matter. He claims to be a humorist, and apparently he is. It says right in his bio link that his humor column, *Joe Ditzel Has Some Problems*, is syndicated worldwide. Some of these columns are about golf. He calls that section *Wasted Mulligan*. You know what? It's pretty funny, and he offers a link to his favorite golf jokes.

17

5 of the Worst Titles of Any Kind

The idea here is bad titles, not necessarily bad content. Bad titles: not catchy, not even kitschy, plain, bland, boring, maybe even dumb. I don't know much about the content of any of these items. Just the titles are bad.

This Title Stinks!

1. *Golf's Mental Magic,* by Dr. Guy S. Fasciana

Huh? Golf makes you mental? Magically? Golfers know a lot of golf is mental, but we've never thought of it as magical. Hard work, yes. Magic, no.

2. *Bet on Your Golf Game! An Indispensable Guide for Betting on the Golf Course,* by Ralph Monti

Here's what the world needs: more ways for poor saps to lose their money. As if greens fees weren't high enough. I wonder if Gamblers Anonymous has this title on its book club list.

3. *Golf Is a Funny Game...but It Wasn't Meant to Be,* by Ken Janke

You darned right it wasn't. This is actually an interesting collection of quotes and thoughts on the game from famous folks. Good book. Bad title.

4. *Holographic Golf: Uniting the Mind and Body to Improve Your Game,* by Larry Miller, cassette tape.

Come now, really? How about "holographing" to find the Holy Grail, too?

5. *Young Golfers Training Kit,* by the PGA; video, coloring and activity book, and crayons.

This is a great idea, only it sounds like they're sending kids to reform school or off to toilet training, not golf fun school.

Section  IV
Golfers

18

20 Wealthiest (Prize-Winning) Male Golfers

When is a dollar not a dollar? When you're comparing what today's athletes earn with their forebears. The inimitable Tiger Woods has won far more money in his few years on the Tour than earlier greats won in a lifetime while winning many more tournaments than the Great New One.

But, it's not only a function of money. The pros also play many more tournaments per year these days. All in all, sometimes numbers lie; well, if they don't lie, they tell half truths.

Check out the postscript list that follows this Top 20. You'll find some amazing names with some surprisingly low totals and rankings.

1.	Tiger Woods	$19,601,950
2.	Davis Love III	$14,619,961
3.	Greg Norman	$13,087,832
4.	Nick Price	$12,771,503
5.	Phil Mickelson	$12,534,115
6.	David Duval	$12,330,792
7.	Fred Couples	$12,254,484

8.	Hal Sutton	$12,077,000
9.	Payne Stewart	$11,737,008
10.	Scott Hoch	$11,605,057
11.	Mark O'Meara	$11,586,578
12.	Mark Calcavecchia	$11,184,440
13.	Tom Kite	$10,654,707
14.	Vijay Singh	$10,497,157
15.	Tom Lehman	$10,082,736
16.	Paul Azinger	$ 9,975,501
17.	Tom Watson	$ 9,583,681
18.	Ernie Els	$ 9,418,512
19.	Loren Roberts	$ 9,199,413
20.	Corey Pavin	$ 9,077,769

And now those low-ranking names...

54.	Jack Nicklaus	$ 5,713,991
149.	Calvin Peete	$ 2,302,363
179.	Arnold Palmer	$ 1,861,857
180.	Gary Player	$ 1,834,482
315.	Sam Snead	$ 620,126

20 Wealthiest (Prize-Winning) Female Golfers

H ere, again, a list that shows dollars aren't what they used to be. But one aspect of these numbers isn't a half truth: The women historically have earned far less prize money than the men. So what else is new?

1.	Betsy King	$6,811,178
2.	Annika Sorenstam	$6,129,096
3.	Juli Inkster	$6,034,775
4.	Karrie Webb	$6,029,095
5.	Beth Daniel	$5,978,378
6.	Pat Bradley	$5,734,628
7.	Dottie Pepper	$5,591,631
8.	Patty Sheehan	$5,500,983
9.	Meg Mallon	$5,434,736
10.	Nancy Lopez	$5,292,645
11.	Laura Davies	$5,171,376
12.	Rosie Jones	$4,859,204
13.	Liselotte Neumann	$4,015,002

14.	Kelly Robbins	$3,933,828
15.	Jane Geddes	$3,705,450
16.	Sherri Steinhauer	$3,595,746
17.	Tammie Green	$3,380,028
18.	Amy Alcott	$3,368,340
19.	Chris Johnson	$3,360,592
20.	Brandie Burton	$3,136,669

...and, again, some big names surprisingly far down the list:

48.	Kathy Whitworth	$1,731,770
191.	Mickey Wright	$ 368,770
258.	Patty Berg	$ 190,760

The 5 Oldest Golfers to Win PGA Tournaments

In this culture that so worships youth, it's nice to know that some folks age gracefully, and maybe even get better with time. Here are five guys who took victory over their younger and more vigorous competitors while well into their middle age. Maybe life indeed can begin at 40.

1. **Sam Snead** was 52 years, 10 months, and 8 days old when he won the Greater Greensboro Open in 1965.
2. **Art Wall** was 51 years, 7 months, and 10 days old when he won the Greater Milwaukee Open in 1975.
3. **Jim Barnes** was 51 years, 3 months, and 7 days old when he won the Long Island Open in 1937.
4. **John Barnum** was 51 years, 1 month, and 5 days old when he won the Cajun Classic in 1962.
5. **Ray Floyd** was 49 years, 6 months, and 4 days old when he won the Doral-Ryder Open in 1992.

And, by the way, when Barnum won the Cajun Classic, he also earned the right to be called the oldest first-time winner on the PGA Tour.

Speaking of age, we know these questions are burning in your brain after reading the old-guys' list:

Q. Who won the most tournaments while in his 30s?

A. Tie: Arnold Palmer and Ben Hogan each won 40 times.

Q. Who won the most tournaments while in his 40s?

A. Slammin' Sammy Snead: He won 17 times in "middle age."

21

10 PGA Tournaments Won by the Youngest Players

There's one guy on this list who you will surely find inspiring. Ray Floyd. Why? He makes the oldest and youngest winners lists, and that's something that bespeaks an extended and productive life. And probably a happy one, too. Everyone likes longevity.

1. **Johnny McDermott** was 19 years and 10 months old when he won the U.S. Open in 1911.

2. **Gene Sarazen** was 20 years and 5 days old when he won the Southern Open in 1922.

3. **Charles Evans**, Jr. was 20 years, 1 month, and 15 days old when he won the Western Open in 1910. He was an amateur, too!

4. **Francis Ouimet** was 20 years, 4 months, and 13 days old when he won the U.S. Open in 1913, and he also was an amateur!

5. **Gene Sarazen** was 20 years, 4 months, and 18 days old when he won again in 1922, this time at the U.S. Open.

6. **Horton Smith** was 20 years, 5 months, and 13 days old when he won the Oklahoma City Open in 1928.

7. **Gene Sarazen** did it again when he was 20 years, 5 months, and 22 days old and won the 1922 PGA.

8. **Raymond Floyd** was 20 years, 6 months, and 13 days old when he won the St. Petersburg Open in 1963.

9. **Phil Mickelson** was 20 years, 6 months, and 28 days old when he won the Northern Telecom Open in 1991. He, too, was an amateur when he did it.

10. **Horton Smith** was 20 years, 7 months, and 1 day old when he won the Catalina Island Open in 1928.

Top 5 Male Golfers of All Time

Oh, isn't this asking for trouble? This list, right here and right now, is going to name the greatest who ever played the game. Is that nerve, or what? Stupidity maybe? Well, before you start throwing things, remember that this is strictly a matter of opinion. Well-educated, well-reasoned opinion, but opinion nonetheless.

1. Jack Nicklaus

Here's a guy who had 71 tour victories, finished second 58 times, and earned a mere 36 third-place finishes, while amassing 100 total victories in world competition. He was the Tour's top money winner eight times and still ranks first with 18 Major Championships, plus six on the Senior PGA Tour, and two Amateurs. He's been honored as the Greatest Golfer and/or Athlete by at least nine publications or broadcast networks and was the *Golf Magazine* and the *Golf Monthly U.K.* "Golfer of the Century."

Maybe the guy could play.

But, beyond that, he became—until the rise of Tiger Woods—symbolic of golf and, along with Arnold Palmer, the driving force behind golf's growing popularity throughout the 1960s and 70s, particularly the sport's increased television coverage.

2. Arnold Palmer

Hey, any guy born in Latrobe, Pennsylvania, must be okay. Folks are probably weaned on Rolling Rock beer out there.

It was Palmer, and his eventual rivalry with Jack Nicklaus, that spawned the television generation of golf fans. The result: his famous "Arnie's Army," who arrived at tournaments by the thousands and sometimes put decorum aside in their enthusiasm for the man. He won the British Open twice, the U.S. Open once, and the Masters four times. But, as much as anything, his product endorsements and earnings from them probably made him the first truly "modern" golf hero.

3. Tiger Woods

In the greater scheme of things, Tiger Woods is still a baby. But even if he walks off the course tomorrow and never comes back, his impact on golf, and on the public's awareness of golf, will rank with the greatest of the greats. Here is a kid who was on television at age two, putting with Bob Hope, and who shot 48 for nine holes at age three.

Of course, the man's accomplishments have been over-documented (this is the age of electronic communication, after all), from his multiple U.S. Amateur victories to his stunning victories in—to date—three Majors. All his accumulative feats have set records or near-records for being the youngest person to accomplish them. But here's the one statistic relevant to his pro career that I like best: As of this writing, the man has missed only one cut in 48 tour events. (It was the 1997 Bell Canadian Open.) Hat's off to the Tiger.

4. Bobby Jones

Jones played his first major tournament, the U.S. Amateur, when he was 14, and finished in the top 10. In all, he won the British Open three times, the British Amateur once, and the U.S. Open and U.S. Amateur four times each. (Remember, in his day, the U.S. and British Amateurs were considered to be Majors.) Most impressive about him, of course, is that he's the only golfer to win all the Majors in a single year. Moreover, as an amateur, he devoted just three months of every year to golf, using the rest of his time to gain high honors while earning degrees in law, English literature, and mechanical engineering, each from a different university.

Then, having won everything there was to win, and having done it more than once, he walked away at the height of his career to begin a successful law practice. Imagine any major athlete doing that today.

5. Gene Sarazen

Here's a guy who only had 18 Tour wins. But seven of those were Majors. He's credited with inventing the sand wedge (he simply soldered extra metal to his niblick to make its sole heavier and broader), and he went on to become a legend in his own time. He was the first player to win all four professional Major championships (when he won the second-ever Masters with his amazing double-eagle two on the 15th—see Chapter 39) and he managed a hole-in-one at age 71 at the 1973 British Open. You've got to love the guy.

Top 5 Female Golfers of All Time

N ow, with the same opinionated-ness and audacity as in Chapter 22, here are the top five ladies.

1. Babe Didriksen Zaharias

Babe Didriksen Zaharias was not only a great golfer, she was the greatest female athlete ever. She gained world fame in track and field and All-American status in basketball; she was a standout in tennis, baseball, softball, diving, roller skating, and even bowling. She held or tied for the world record in the javelin throw, 80-meter hurdles, high jump, and long jump, won two gold medals and one silver in the 1932 Olympics, and earlier that same year, not only won eight of 10 events in the AAU's National Women's Track and Field Championship, but won the team competition as a one-woman team. She was named the Associated Press (AP) Woman Athlete of the Year in 1931, 1945, 1946, 1947, 1950, and 1954. She was subsequently voted the AP Woman Athlete of the First Half of the 20th Century.

But could she play golf? How about 41 career victories, including 10 Majors (four as an amateur)? How about three LPGA Majors in 1950 alone, and from 1950 to 1951 leading the LPGA in money earnings? She was named "Golfer of the Decade" by

Golf Magazine for the years 1948 to 1957; she was *Sports Illustrated's* Individual Female Athlete of the Century and the AP Top Woman Athlete of the Century, both in 1999. She was one of the six inaugural inductees into the LPGA Tour Hall of Fame.

She was, simply, the greatest.

2. Kathy Whitworth

Between 1958 and 1985, Kathy Whitworth amassed fully 88 career victories (more than any other professional golfer in history, male or female), including six Majors. Not bad, eh? She was named AP Athlete of the Year in 1965 and 1967, and she was named "Golfer of the Decade" by *Golf Magazine* for the years 1968 to 1977. She's a proud member of the New Mexico Hall of Fame, Texas Sports and Golf Hall of Fame, World Golf Hall of Fame, and the Women's Sports Foundation Hall of Fame.

3. Mickey Wright

How can you not love a woman named Mickey? Mary Kathryn Wright won the 1952 U.S. Girls' Amateur, then turned pro and immediately continued winning. But in 1958, she *really* started winning, taking the U.S. Women's Open and the LPGA Championship that year. From 1958 to 1964, she won eight Majors, topping the money list from 1961 to 1964. In 1963 alone she had 13 victories in 32 tournaments; no one has ever topped that. She won 82 LPGA tournaments in all, won the Vare Trophy five times, was the leading money winner four times, twice had four-tournament winning streaks, and was named the AP Woman Athlete of the Year twice. A winner.

4. Nancy Lopez

It's true. I love Nancy Lopez because she's married to Ray Knight, who was instrumental in bringing the N.Y. Mets their 1986 World Series victory. But, she's also a great golfer. As of press time, she's earned 48 career victories, won three Majors, and ranks fifth in career earnings. She was named Golfer of the Decade by *Golf Magazine* for the years 1978 to 1987, and she was honored with the USGA's 1998 Bob Jones Award, which recognizes distinguished sportsmanship in the game of golf. She simply dominated women's golf during the 1970s and 1980s, and was inducted into the PGA Hall of Fame in 1989. She's the only player to win the Rolex Rookie of the Year, the Rolex Player of the Year, and the Vare Trophy in the same season.

Now, if she'd only get Ray to come back and lead the Mets to another Series win.

5. Joyce Wethered

Back in a time when it wasn't particularly common to be a female golfer, there was Joyce Wethered. Back in a time when money was never on the line, Joyce Wethered won five English Amateurs and four British Ladies Amateurs. She won her first in 1920 and quit just nine years later. That's a lot of wins in a short time. Bobby Jones said of her, "I have never played against anyone and felt so outclassed." Indeed, Jones is reputed to have regarded her as the finest golfer, man or woman, he had ever seen. And that's a good enough judge of greatness for me.

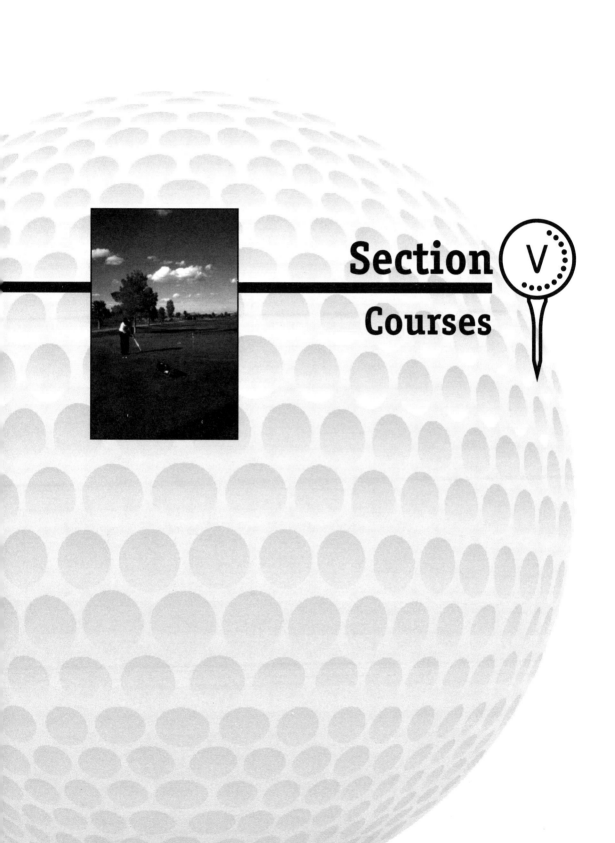

Section V

Courses

12 Best Public Golf Courses in the English-Speaking World

This list is restricted to courses the public can play; the heck with snobs who hoard their challenges to themselves. Of course, listing 12 courses as "the best" is absurd. But, then again, so is trying to hit a small sphere into a hole in the ground 500 yards away. I'm sure that each of you out there has a gripe with these choices. How could [insert course name] be included? How could [insert course name] be omitted? I'll tell you how: because the list was restricted to 12, that's how!

1. Pebble Beach (Golf Links Course), Pebble Beach, California

No doubt one of the world's best-known courses, if for no other reason than Bob Hope made it famous with his tournament. But, the truth is, it's a hell of a course. It challenges you with teeny greens, narrow fairways, and deep, deep rough. The ocean views are terrific, and that ocean is hungry to devour your errant shots. And, of course, where there's ocean, there will be wind. Eighteen— a par-5 that hugs the precipitously rocky shoreline—stands among the most famous finishing holes, if the course hasn't finished you first.

- Address: 1700 17 Mile Drive, Pebble Beach, CA 93953
- Phone: 831-625-8518 (Pro Shop)
- Web site: *www.pebblebeach.com*

- Yardage: 6719
- Par: 72
- Rating: 73.8
- Slope: 142
- Greens Fee: $305

2. St. Andrews (Old Course), Fife, Scotland

This is an obvious one. Bow three times in its direction. If you play golf at all, you want to play here. Why not? Folks have been doing it since 1522. There are six 18-hole courses here, but the Old Course is the original. It runs up and back on a sandy, dune filled, narrow strip of land along the wind-ripped, stormy North Sea. After you've fought the elements and the natural terrain almost all the way through, you get to play the 17th hole, where most of us would find ourselves in the Road Hole bunker; that is, playing from the road.

- Address: Pilmour House, St Andrews, Fife KY16 9SF, Scotland, UK
- Phone: +44 (0) 1334 466666
- Web site: *www.standrews.org.uk*
- Yardage: 6566
- Par: 72
- Greens Fee: £60-£85

3. Pinehurst (No. 2), Pinehurst, North Carolina

Another legendary location for smacking small spheres, which they've been doing here since 1894. Number 2 is, of course, the famous one because Majors have been played on it, but the resort actually contains eight outstanding golf courses. The salient features of Number 2—indeed of each Pinehurst course—are the big-time rough, sand aplenty, tree-lined fairways, and big old nature intruding into play all over the place. On Number 2, fame also derives from the greens, those upside-down saucers enveloped by dips and hollows. Bring your short game, as they say, if you have one. They also say you'll rarely lose a ball here—no water or tight trees—but they've never played with the likes of me.

- Address: Carolina Vista Drive, Pinehurst, NC 28374
- Phone: 910-295-8141 (Pro Shop)
- Yardage: 7252
- Par: 72
- Rating: 75.9
- Slope: 138
- Greens Fee: $275

4. Ballybunion (Old Course), County Kerry, Ireland

Ah, golf in Ireland. Nothing quite so absurd, unless it's golf in Scotland. Dunes, hillocks, ocean, erratic winds: It all adds up to someone's definition of fun. Ballybunion, among Ireland's best, is no exception. It sits seaside. Its dunes tower at right angles to the water. Impossible crosswinds flurry shots all over the place. You get the picture.

- Address: Sandhill Road, Ballybunion, Co Kerry, Ireland
- Phone: +353 (0) 68 27146
- Web site: *www.ballybuniongolfclub.ie*
- Yardage: 6603
- Par: 71
- Greens Fee: £75

5. Carnoustie (Championship Course), Angus, Scotland

Now, if you like all the above-mentioned elements, particularly the windy bit (as residents of the British Isles would say), Carnoustie's for you. Many consider it to be among the greatest links-style courses in the world. The Championship Course features a notorious wind-swept opening hole, and the famous "sting-in-the-tail" closing holes. You may not go home stung, but there's a good chance your tail will be between your legs.

- Address: Links Parade, Carnoustie, Angus DD77JE, Scotland
- Phone: +44 (0)1241 853249
- Web site: *www.carnoustie.org*
- Yardage: 6941
- Par: 75
- Greens Fee: £36

6. Harbour Town Golf Links Course at Sea Pines Resort, Hilton Head Island, South Carolina

They play the MCI Heritage Classic here, but that's not what makes it great. The fairways are lined by pines and live oaks, but that doesn't make it great either. The greens are suitably small, but greatness isn't created that way. Here, too, the 18th hole is the flashy centerfold hole, where a mistake lands you in Calibogue Sound. But, neither is that what makes it great, at least not in my opinion. I think it's the par-threes, which are some of the prettiest, gnarliest, most teasing, and most rewarding par-threes ever seen. Add the par-threes to all the other factors, and now you've got greatness.

- Address: 32 Greenwood Drive, Hilton Head Island, SC 29928
- Phone: 888-807-6873 or 800-925-4653
- Web site: *www.seapines.com*
- Yardage: 6916
- Par: 71
- Rating: 74.0
- Slope: 136
- Greens Fee: $225

7. Bay Harbor Golf Club (Links/Quarry Course), Bay Harbor, Michigan

You make 18 here by playing two of their three nines. The Links/Quarry combination gets the nod as best. Now, unless you're from Michigan, you probably don't think of the state as coastal. But there's this little body of water called Lake Michigan that makes it so and, if you play all 27 holes at Bay Harbor, you'll be playing the longest golf course coastline in America. The topography varies greatly. The Links traverses bluffs high above the lake. The Quarry Course is surrounded by cliffs. Any way you cut it, however, this is a course to be reckoned with and revered.

- Address: 5800 Coastal Ridge Drive, Bay Harbor, MI 49770
- Phone: 888-229-4272 or 231-439-4028
- Web site: *www.bayharbor.com*
- Yardage: 6780
- Par: 72
- Rating: 72.2
- Slope: 143
- Greens Fee: $240

8. The Challenge at Manele, Lanai City, Lanai, Hawaii

Lava captures the imagination, and this course is built on lava outflows. Toss in the exotic-sounding Kiawe and wild Llima trees, add a hilly oceanside layout, mix with small canyons that must be hit across to reach the fairways and, as ever with oceanside sites, give us some hearty winds, and you've got some mighty golfing indeed. I like the variety of blind tee and approach shots, the over-the-ocean shots required along the way, and of course just the idea of being in Hawaii.

- Address: 1233 Fraser Avenue, Lanai City, Lanai, HI 96763
- Phone: 800-321-4666 or 808-565-2222
- Web site: *www.lanai-resorts.com/golf.html*
- Yardage: 7039
- Par: 72
- Rating: 73.3
- Slope: 132
- Greens Fee: $145 (hotel guest) $200 (non-guest)

9. Kemper Lakes Golf Club, Long Grove, Illinois

You can play golf in many exotic places, and Illinois is one of them. This is the site of the Grand Slam of Golf from 1986 to 1990 and the home of the Illinois PGA. Not to be outdone by the ocean brought into play in places like Pebble Beach and Hawaii, here in the nation's breadbasket we find a remarkable amount of water in the form of lakes. In at least one case, the third hole, you must play over the H_2O. Narrow fairways add to the fun. It's said that the 16th hole, a 469-yard, par-4, is considered the toughest on the PGA Senior Tour.

- Address: Old McHenry Road, Long Grove, IL 60049
- Phone: 847-320-3450
- Web site: *www.kemperlakesgolf.com*
- Yardage: 7217
- Par: 72
- Rating: 75.9
- Slope: 143
- Greens Fee: $130

10. Portmarnock Golf Club, County Dublin, Ireland

Ireland's finest, it's a links course that's laid out in loops, meaning you have to play the wind in all directions. The sixth hole pushes 600 yards with water in play.

- Address: Portmarnock, Co Dublin, Ireland
- Phone: +353 (0) 01-8462968
- Web site: *www.portmarnockgolfclub.ie*
- Yardage: 7182
- Par: 72
- Greens Fee: £70.00-£90.00

11. Bethpage State Park (The Black Course), Farmingdale, New York

"Babe," Moe Stooge said to the beautiful young girl, "Let me take you away to the islands—the exotic isles of Coney and Long." Don't know what Moe had in mind, but a stop at Bethpage probably was on his itinerary. You don't think of Long Island, New York, as topographically dynamic, but here you find hills galore, which yield in turn uneven lies galore. The rough along the fairways is very deep, and locals say it's a long way from the tees to the greens. It may be, but it's also a long way to Tipperary, and eventually folks who have the desire and skills get there.

- Address: Bethpage State Park, Farmingdale, NY 11735
- Phone: 516-249-4040
- Yardage: 7065
- Par: 71

- Rating: 75.4
- Slope: 144
- Greens Fee: $31 (weekday); $39 (weekends)

12. Sugarloaf Golf Club & Resort, Kingfield, Maine

If you've ever skied Sugarloaf, you know it's one heck of a hill. And this is one heck of a golf course. Up and down, up and down. Is this golf or mountain climbing? But, unlike playing mountain courses out West, you don't get what is called the "elevation advantage," where the ball flies a million times farther because of the altitude. Here in Maine, you get great mountain views without needing supplemental oxygen. Eleven is the signature hole: a 222-yard, par-3, with a tee shot from a cliff, over a river, through the woods (but not to Grandmother's house), to the green.

- Address: Route 1, Kingfield, ME 04947
- Phone: 800-843-5623 or 207-237-2000
- Web site: *www.sugarloaf.com*
- Yardage: 6956
- Par: 72
- Rating: 74.4
- Slope: 151
- Greens Fee: $99

6 Most Beautiful Courses in the United States

Oh boy. Now I've opened up a can of worms. Who decides what's beautiful? What are the criteria? Well, you'll notice a bias towards waterside and mountain courses here. Sorry if you prefer the desert or suburbia, but I'm making the decisions. And I think I know a beautiful golf course when I see one, or just pictures of one.

1. Prince Course at Princeville Golf and Country Club, Kauai, Hawaii

A Scottish links-style course in the south Pacific. Isn't cross-culturing wonderful? Here, you get the best of Hawaiian scenery and views, matched with a magnificent layout and some wonderful natural hazards in play, like Anini Stream. In some spots, magnificent beach and rolling surf dazzle the eye. Then,

on holes like Number 12, you encounter sights like a 100-foot elevated tee and a hole that plays through a mango grove. Add some cliffs here and there and—voila!—beautiful.

- Address: Kauai, HI 96722
- Phone: 800-826-4400 or 808-826-9644
- Web site: *www.princeville.com*
- Yardage: 7309
- Par: 72
- Rating: 75.3
- Slope: 145
- Greens Fee: $155

2. Bandon Dunes, Bandon, Oregon

The Oregon coast may be the most beautiful coastline in the country: rugged, wild, unruly, and awe inspiring. This is a must-walk, Scottish-links-style course that sits about 100 miles north of the California border. You'll deal with wind and fog, but the dunes and indigenous vegetation have  been left untouched, and the sense of grandeur is almost eerie.

- Address: 57744 Round Lake Drive, Bandon, OR 97411
- Phone: 888-345-6008 or 541-347-4380
- Web site: *www.bandondunesgolf.com*
- Yardage: 6844
- Par: 72
- Rating: 74.2
- Slope: 138
- Greens Fee: $100

3. Pasatiempo Golf Club, Santa Cruz, California

Another seaside course, this is an Alister MacKenzie design on which steep barranca runs through the back nine. You get trees, rolling hills, and a sophisticated but rough sensibility that only the northern California coast can evoke.

- Address: 18 Clubhouse Road, Santa Cruz, CA 95060
- Phone: 831-459-9193 or 831-459-9155
- Web site: *www.pasatiempo.com*
- Yardage: 6445
- Par: 72
- Rating: 72.9
- Slope: 138
- Greens Fee: $115-$125

4. Greenbrier Course at The Greenbrier Resort, White Sulphur Springs, West Virginia

This mountain course offers only moderately rolling terrain, but simply marvelous panoramic Allegheny Mountains views.

- Address: 300 W Main Street, White Sulphur Springs, WV 24986
- Phone: 800 453-4858 or 304-536-7834
- Web site: *www.greenbrier.com*
- Yardage: 6675
- Par: 72
- Rating: 73.1
- Slope: 135
- Greens Fee: $135

5. Pebble Beach (Golf Links Course), Pebble Beach, California

This one keeps cropping up on all the lists, doesn't it?

- Address: 1700 17 Mile Drive, Pebble Beach, CA 93953
- Phone: 831-625-8518 (Pro Shop)
- Web site: *www.pebblebeach.com*
- Yardage: 6719

- Par: 72
- Rating: 73.8
- Slope: 142
- Greens Fee: $305

6. Estes Park Golf Course, Estes Park, Colorado

This isn't a fancy resort with a special name designer. It is just a public golf course in one of the most beautiful settings anywhere: adjoining Rocky Mountain National Park. Set at a 7,500-foot elevation, the course sits in a valley surrounded by spectacular mountains and is often visited by deer, elk, and even coyote. This happens to be *my* idea of paradise.

- Address: 1080 S Saint Vraine Avenue, Estes Park, CO 80517
- Phone: 970-586-8146
- Web site: *www.estesvalleyrecreation.com*
- Yardage: 6321
- Par: 71
- Rating: 68.3
- Slope: 118
- Greens Fee: $33

5 Most Beautiful Courses in the World

Beauty, they say, is in the eye of the beholder. The courses on this list are the most beautiful. They are exotic, visually striking, and all foreign.

1. Bali Handara Country Club, Pancasari, Bali, Indonesia

This is a truly exotic golf resort in a truly exotic place: the Alpine highlands of Bali. The course sits at the mouth of an extinct volcano and is rimmed by rain forest. The views are incredible. Mount Penanggungan looms in the background and, from various elevated tees, the 700-year-old Candi Jawi Temple is revealed. Besides, how many times do you get to play shots over rice paddies?

- Address: P.O. 324 Denpasar, Pancasari, Bali, Indonesia
- Phone: 062-0361-28866
- Yardage: 7024
- Par: 72
- Greens Fee: $20-$34 (guests); $39-61 (non-guests)

2. Kawana Hotel, North Shizuoka Prefecture, Japan

Set on the Izu Peninsula, this resort gives you all the visual wonder of a rocky seaside course with the full Japanese treatment in design, service, and amenities.

This is another place where you'd have to pinch yourself to make sure you weren't dreaming. Choose either of the two courses, and let your eye be dazzled.

- Address: 1459 Kawana, No. Shizuoka Prefecture, Japan
- Phone: 800-526-2281 or 081-0557-45-1111
- Web site: *www.kawana-hotel.com/english*
- Yardage: 5,711 (Oshima Course) or 6,691 (Fuji Course)
- Par: 70/72
- Greens Fee: 26,495-30,445 (Japanese Yen)

3. Banff Springs Hotel, Banff, Alberta, Canada

There may be no scenery in North America to match the Canadian Rockies. Here's a course that sits tidily under the magnificent Mt. Rundle within the expansive confines of Banff National Park, with the 19th-century Scottish Baronial castle-style Banff Springs Hotel lording over all. Breathtaking is the only way to describe this setting.

- Address: 405 Spray Avenue, Banff, Alberta T0L 0C0, Canada
- Phone: 800-441-1414 or 403-762-2211
- Web site: *www.cphotels.com*
- Yardage: 7083
- Par: 71
- Rating: 74.4
- Slope: 142
- Greens Fee: $150 (Canadian dollars)

4. The Tryall Club, Sandy Bay, Jamaica

Jamaica may be the best of all Caribbean settings because it has a complete topography: ocean, wetlands, forests, and mountains. The Tryall Club sits about

12 miles west of Montego Bay in a fantastically lush tropical setting. If one must leave the mountains, this is the kind of place to be.

- Address: Sandy Bay, Jamaica
- Phone: 800-336-4571 or 809-956-5660
- Web site: *www.tryallclub.com*
- Yardage: 6407
- Par: 71
- Rating: 72.5
- Slope: 133
- Greens Fee: $40-$80

5. Sheraton Mirage at Port Douglas, Port Douglas, Queensland, Australia

Maybe it's just my fascination with the Great Barrier Reef and the Coral Sea, but I don't think seaside settings get more magnificent than this.

- Address: Davidson Street, P.O. Box 172, Port Douglas, Queensland 4871, Australia
- Phone: 617-4099-5888
- Web site: *www.sheraton-mirage.com*
- Yardage: 6847
- Par: 71
- Greens Fee: Contact the resort

10 Most Difficult Courses in the English-Speaking World

This was another difficult list to compile.

1. St. Andrews (Old Course), Fife, Scotland

This choice is based partially on reputation and pure heritage (no world "best" list of any kind should be without St. Andrews), and partially on the wind. If you can play this place without the ghosts getting to you, and without the wind making you crazy, you're some kind of good golfer.

RULE XXXII
A player may stand out of bounds to play a ball lying within bounds.

- Address: Pilmour House, St Andrews, Fife KY16 9SF, Scotland, UK

- Phone: +44 (0) 1334 466666
- Web site: *www.standrews.org.uk*
- Yardage: 6566
- Par: 72
- Greens Fee: £60-£85

2. Pebble Beach (Golf Links Course), Pebble Beach, California

Here's another one based on reputation and history. Still, you may be driven to suicide by diving off the cliffs and into the rocks as you follow your ball to the ocean.

- Address: 1700 17 Mile Drive, Pebble Beach, CA 93953
- Phone: 831-625-8518 (Pro Shop)
- Web site: *www.pebblebeach.com*
- Yardage: 6719
- Par: 72
- Rating: 73.8
- Slope: 142
- Greens Fee: $305

3. Harbour Town Golf Links Course at Sea Pines Resort, Hilton Head Island, South Carolina

This is a pretty tight course, all in all. It features plenty of marsh into which to drive, chip, or otherwise play your shots; good cross winds on the finishing hole; and some par-three's with pot-hole bunkers that invite you to burrow underground and not bother coming up for air…ever.

- Address: 32 Greenwood Drive, Hilton Head Island, SC 29928
- Phone: 888-807-6873
  or 800-925-4653
- Web site: *www.seapines.com*
- Yardage: 6916
- Par: 71
- Rating: 74.0
- Slope: 136
- Greens Fee: $225

4. Pinehurst (No. 2), Pinehurst, North Carolina

Here's another famous one. Even the pros will tell you that Number 2 looks easy, but the trouble is, it isn't. Despite the lack of tricks, trees, and other annoyances, it somehow makes an honest man or woman out of you, all the while lulling you into a false sense of security.

- Address: Carolina Vista Drive, Pinehurst, NC 28374
- Phone: 910-295-8141 (Pro Shop)
- Yardage: 7252
- Par: 72
- Rating: 75.9
- Slope: 138
- Greens Fee: $275

5. Sugarloaf Golf Club and Resort, Kingfield, Maine

Many folks have called this the best resort/mountain course in the country. To really prove it to yourself, walk it. You can then apply for a diploma from mountain-climbing school. The course is hilly, and it's a terrific challenge.

- Address: Route 1, Kingfield, ME 04947
- Phone: 800-843-5623 or 207-237-2000
- Web site: *www.sugarloaf.com*
- Yardage: 6956
- Par: 72
- Rating: 74.4
- Slope: 151
- Greens Fee: $99

6. Le Manoir Richelieu, Pointe-au-Pic, Quebec, Canada

Charlevoix, east of Quebec City, is a too-often overlooked region of Quebec Province, but it's among the most beautiful parts of Canada, and this course is both beautiful and challenging. Once a favorite haunt of president William H. Taft, it sits high above the St. Lawrence River from whence it rambles, tumbles, and plays just plain ornery with major elevation changes on every hole. Plus, you can practice your French without going overseas.

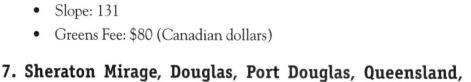

RULE 1 Definition.
(h) Casual water is any temporary accumulation of water...which is not one of the ordinary... hazards of the course.

The Rules of Golf

- Address: 181, rue Richelieu, La Malbaie, Charlevoix, Quebec G5A 1X7, Canada
- Phone: 800-441-1414 or 418-665-3703
- Web site: *www.fairmont.com*
- Yardage: 6220
- Par: 71
- Rating: 70.0
- Slope: 131
- Greens Fee: $80 (Canadian dollars)

7. Sheraton Mirage, Douglas, Port Douglas, Queensland, Australia

You're playing here along the Great Barrier Reef and the Coral Sea. That distraction alone will make it a difficult day.

- Address: Davidson Street, P.O. Box 172, Port Douglas, Queensland 4871, Australia
- Phone: 617-4099-5888
- Web site: *www.sheraton-mirage.com*
- Yardage: 6847

- Par: 71
- Greens Fee: Contact the resort.

8. Kiawah Island Resort, Kiawah Island, South Carolina

They've played Ryder Cup Matches on the Ocean Course. But that beautiful ocean eats balls, and plenty of them, and the tight layout demands not only skill but that you be honest about yourself. Rationalizing lies about your skills will soon be revealed here.

- Address: 1000 Ocean Course Drive, Kiawah Island, SC 29455
- Phone: 800-576-1500 or 843-768-2121
- Web site: *www.kiawahgolf.com*
- Yardage: 7296
- Par: 72
- Rating: 78.0
- Slope: 152
- Greens Fee: $225

9. Mauna Kea Course, Mauna Kea Beach Hotel, Kohala Coast, Hawaii

This Robert Trent Jones, Sr. course, like the Sirens of Greek legend, is almost universally considered to hold a lethal combination: unmarred beauty and alarmingly serious challenge. First it seduces you, then it renders you useless.

- Address: 62-100 Mauna Kea Beach Drive, Kamuela, HI 96743
- Phone: 800-882-6060 or 808-882-5400
- Web site: *www.maunakeabeachhotel.com*
- Yardage: 7114
- Par: 72
- Rating: 73.6
- Slope: 143
- Greens Fee: $175

10. Cascades Golf Club, Hot Springs, Virginia

Another mountain setting, this course belongs to the classy Homestead Resort. Narrow fairways lined by very large trees, plenty of natural water hazards, abundant uneven lies, and subtly breaking greens combine to make the challenge here. And, why not? The course opened in 1923, when men were men and golf was supposed to be confounding. Right?

- Address: Route 2, Hot Springs, VA 24445
- Phone: 800-838-1766 or 540-839-3083
- Web site: *www.thehomestead.com*
- Yardage: 6659
- Par: 70
- Rating: 72.9
- Slope: 136
- Greens Fee: $150

Top Courses in the United States by Region

J ust to prolong the controversy—or perhaps to have more fun with it—here is a list of three favorite courses in each region within the contiguous United States. The list is steered toward the interesting, not necessarily the glamorous, and the dynamic instead of the obvious.

Northeast

1. Blue Heron Pines Golf Club, Cologne, New Jersey

South central New Jersey's finest, it's a daily-fee course. Stephen Kay did the design, and he does the wetlands and semi-coastal topography of south New Jersey complete justice.

- Address: 550 W Country Club Drive, Cologne, NJ 08213
- Phone: 609-965-4653
- Web site: *www.blueheronpines.com*
- Yardage: 6777
- Par: 72
- Rating: 72.9
- Slope: 132
- Greens Fee: $99-$125

2. Green Mountain National, Killington, Vermont

When Killington ski resort built its course years back, the complaint came that it was just too hilly. Now comes this course, a few miles up Route 100 from the ski area: tree-lined fairways and a course that wends its way through granite ledges and wetlands bits, requiring fine shotmaking and revealing terrific mountain views without having to actually climb, although you'll get your share of elevation changes on the back nine.

- Address: Barrows-Towne Road, Killington, VT 05751
- Phone: 802-422-4653
- Web site: *www.gmngc.com*
- Yardage: 6589
- Par: 71
- Rating: 72.6
- Slope: 139
- Greens Fee: $52

3. Eagle's Landing, Ocean City, Maryland

This is an actual, real-live municipal golf course. The world needs more of this kind of thing. It starts out pretty easy, but gets more and more challenging as you roll along. You play your way through plenty of marshland that you frequently have to carry; you may want to carry an extra dozen ball sleeves. This was, by the way, the first course in Maryland to be certified as an Audubon Sanctuary.

- Address: 12367 Eagle's Nest Road, Berlin, MD 21811
- Phone: 410-213-7277
- Yardage: 7003
- Par: 72

- Rating: 74.3
- Slope: 126
- Greens Fee: $32

4. Nemacolin Woodlands Resort, Farmington, Pennsylvania

I know, I said only three courses per region. Well, I lied. This is number four for the Northeast. Set in the Laurel Highlands, an often forgotten part of Pennsylvania (especially if you're from the eastern part of the state), here are beautiful, rolling, wooded hills just an hour's drive from Pittsburgh. The course is a Pete Dye creation, one he has commented may be his best, and it cuts through what was heavy-duty rock escarpments. You need to shoot long and straight here. Not only rocks and trees will haunt you, but water shows up at seven greens. Great setting, great challenge, great golf.

- Address: Route 40 E, Farmington, PA 15437
- Phone: 724-329-6111
- Web site: *www.nwlr.com*
- Yardage: 6832
- Par: 72
- Rating: 75.0
- Slope: 146
- Greens Fee: $150

Southeast

1. Cherokee Run, Conyers, Georgia

An Arnold Palmer/Ed Seay design, this is a relatively new club not far from Atlanta. It was the site for two Olympic events of the modern pentathalon, and the equestrian and mountain biking competitions during the 1996 Games. You play among plentiful oaks and dogwoods in the shadow of a rocky outcropping called Stone Mountain. The greens are large and the forced carries few, but imposing rocks, trees, ravines, and a creek make the challenge. The pair of finishing holes take in wetlands, waterfalls, a creek, and some uphill slugging...Olympian stuff, to be sure.

- Address: 1595 Centennial Olympic Parkway, Conyers, GA 30013
- Phone: 770-785-7904

- Web site: *www.cherokeerun.com*
- Yardage: 7016
- Par: 72
- Rating: 74.9
- Slope: 142
- Greens Fee: $45-$65

2. True Blue Golf Club, Pawleys Island, South Carolina

Myrtle Beach offers uninterrupted golf for nearly 60 miles. It can be confusing. But this site on Pawley's Island is away from the mainline and development hubbub. There's lots of sand and waste bunkers, trees, and even railroad tie constructions to play over, around, and through, but the fairways are nice and wide and it's a course that doesn't overwhelm the average golfer. Among the myriad Grand Strand choices, this stands among the better ones.

- Address: 900 Blue Stem Drive, Pawley's Island, SC 29585
- Phone: 888-483-6801
- Web site: *www.truebluegolf.com*
- Yardage: 7060
- Par: 72
- Rating: 73.8
- Slope: 139
- Greens Fee: $100

3. The Colonial Golf Course, Williamsburg, Virginia

The Colonial Golf Course was Williamsburg's first daily-fee facility. Historic Williamsburg is a magnificent place to visit, and it also yields an endlessly fascinating peek into the country's history. After immersing yourself in colonial times, you'll have earned immersion in this rolling, smooth-flowing course. Lots of white oak trees and some beautiful flowering mountain laurels, as well as the picturesque Mill Creek, add dynamism and radiance, but the fairways are wide enough to forgive you—and maybe let you make history of your own.

- Address: 8285 Diascund Road, Williamsburg, VA 23089
- Phone: 800-566-6660 or 757-566-1600
- Web site: *www.golfcolonial.com*
- Yardage: 6885
- Par: 72
- Rating: 73.1
- Slope: 132
- Greens Fee: $80

Midwest

1. The Bear, Grand Traverse Resort, Traverse City, Michigan

They grow a ton of cherries up in Traverse City, and this course is one of them. The admonition to designer Jack Nicklaus was to come up with his toughest course, and he has succeeded. People come from all over the place to answer the challenge of challenging contouring, water, and bunkers. Bring a "go for it" attitude.

- Address: 100 Grand Traverse Village Boulevard, PO Box 404, Acme, Michigan 49610
- Phone: 800-236-1577
- Web site: *www.grandtraverseresort.com*
- Yardage: 7065
- Par: 72
- Rating: 76.8

- Slope: 146
- Greens Fee: $75-$100 (guest); 85-$130 (non-guest)

2. The Heather, Boyne Highlands Resort, Harbor Springs, Michigan

Boyne Highlands is a ski resort. Boyne Highlands is a golf resort. Yes, Boyne's got it all—including this Robert Trent Jones classic. Large greens, long tee boxes, water hazards, stretched bunkers: You play at the base of the ski mountain through forest and blueberry bogs and sometimes maniacal winds. You'll never see another fairway from the one you're playing—something I very much like. Now see if you can get past that lake on Number 18.

- Address: 600 Highland Drive, Harbor Springs, MI 49740
- Phone: 800-462-6963 or 231-526-3000
- Web site: *www.boynehighlands.com*
- Yardage: 7210
- Par: 72
- Rating: 73.7
- Slope: 131
- Greens Fee: $130

3. University Ridge, Verona, Wisconsin

Owned by the University of Wisconsin, this course is schizophrenic. The front nine is almost like playing the wide-open spaces of the prairie. The back nine is tight, densely treed, and even features a split fairway on the 16th hole pocked by 14 bunkers. Yikes.

- Address: 7120 County Trunk Pd, Verona, WI 53593
- Phone: 800-897-4343 or 608-845-7700
- Web site: *www.wisc.edu/ath/facil/uridge/uridge.html*
- Yardage: 6888
- Par: 72
- Rating: 73.2
- Slope: 142
- Greens Fee: $51

Southwest

1. University of New Mexico Championship Course, Albuquerque, New Mexico

Albuquerque is a funny place. A sort of sprawling miniature Los Angeles, it's surrounded by arroyos, mountains, plateaus, and desert. You're playing at 5,000 feet here, so the ball will carry, but you're also playing in a wooded hillside environment that might make you forget you're in the expansive Southwest. The greens are closely guarded, and there's enough undulation in the contours to keep things interesting. After your round, you will be given a college-level exam.

- Address: 2201 Tucker Road NE, Albuquerque, NM 87131
- Phone: 505-277-4146
- Yardage: 6822
- Par: 72
- Rating: 68.8
- Slope: 120
- Greens Fee: $10.50—$11.55

2. Legend Trail, Scottsdale, Arizona

Sooner or later everyone will come to Scottsdale, won't they? This is classic desert golfing, complete with huge Saguaro cacti, boulders, and rugged washes. As if hitting off into the desert itself isn't enough of a problem, you'll find plenty of bunkers in which to ensnare yourself, and, then, in places like the seventh, a waterfall and a small lake, too. Desert, my eye.

- Address: 9462 Legendery Lane, Scottsdale, AZ 85262
- Phone: 480-488-7434
- Web site: *www.troongolf.com*
- Yardage: 6845
- Par: 72
- Rating: 72.3
- Slope: 135
- Greens Fee: $145

3. Karsten Creek, Stillwater, Oklahoma

Although it's true that many of us who live in the East still associate Oklahoma with the Dust Bowl of the 1930s, there is beauty all around in the state, and this is one place you'll find it. Featuring beautiful, narrow fairways with mature trees lining them, hilly terrain, and subtle greens, it is a purist's dream.

- Address: 1800 S Memorial Drive, Stillwater, OK 74074
- Phone: 405-743-1658
- Yardage: 7095
- Par: 72
- Rating: 74.8
- Slope: 142
- Greens Fee: $150

Rocky Mountains

1. Teton Pines, Jackson, Wyoming

The Grand Teton Mountains are as beautiful as any in the country. The cowboy culture remains strong and not overly kitschy. The skiing's great in winter. And this Arnold Palmer and Ed Seay golf course is worthy of the locale. You've got to play around the Snake River here; water comes into play on every hole except Number Two. The course itself is relatively flat, given all the mountains around, but you are playing in the valley, after all. The scenery alone is worth the price of admission.

- Address: 3450 N Clubhouse Drive, Jackson, WY 83001
- Phone: 800-238-2223
- Web site: *www.tetonpines.com*
- Yardage: 7412
- Par: 72
- Rating: 74.8
- Slope: 137
- Greens Fee: $155

2. Old Works, Anaconda, Montana

Built atop a Superfund site where a copper-smelting plant once operated, the course includes a number of historic mining structures, including huge stone furnaces and a 585-foot smokestack. This is all set against a startling mountain backdrop. You also get a creek, four ponds, and bunkers filled with black slag, a normal byproduct of copper smelting.

- Address: 1205 Pizzini Way, Anaconda, MT 59711
- Phone: 406-563-5989
- Web site: *www.oldworks.org*
- Yardage: 7705
- Par: 72
- Rating: 76.6
- Slope: 138
- Greens Fee: $36

3. Championship Course at Buffalo Hill Golf Club, Kalispell, Montana

This odd course, which sits smack in the middle of downtown Kalispell while the Rocky Mountains loom all around you, was first opened in 1929 as a Works Progress Administration (WPA) project. The championship 18 isn't that old, but there's a cozy, homespun feeling to playing here that can't be beat, and the small, elevated greens and tree-lined, hilly fairways demand accuracy.

- Address: N Main Street, Kalispell, MT 59901
- Phone: 406-756-4545
- Yardage: 6584
- Par: 72
- Rating: 71.4
- Slope: 131
- Greens Fee: $33

Northwest

1. Olympic Course at Gold Mountain, Bremerton, Washington

You take the ferry from Seattle to Bremerton—the quintessential Seattle waterborne experience—and then you play this course with 100-foot-tall pines and plentiful lakes and streams. Just watch out for the greens; they are very tricky stuff. This is a municipal course, another factor in its favor.

- Address: 7263 W. Belfair Valley Road, Bremerton, WA 98312
- Phone: 800-249-2363 or 360-674-2363
- Yardage: 7003
- Par: 72
- Rating: 73.1
- Slope: 128
- Greens Fee: $25-$29

2. Crosswater at Sunriver Resort, Sunriver, Oregon

Here in the shadow of Mount Bachelor, one of the Pacific Northwest's best skiing volcanoes, you're actually playing in high desert, surrounded by big time

Ponderosa pines. The trout streams wending their way through the course are almost a cliche, they're so pretty. Crosswater can play as long as 7,683 yards, yet still requires skilled placement and teases shamelessly with its well-protected greens. All as the Deschutes and Little Deschutes Rivers roll along.

- Address: Center Drive, Sunriver, OR 97707
- Phone: 541-593-1221
- Web site: *www.sunriver-resort.com*
- Yardage: 7683
- Par: 72
- Rating: 76.9
- Slope: 150
- Greens Fee: $120-$135

3. Eagle Point Golf Course, Eagle Point, Oregon

If you've never been to Crater Lake National Park, go there first. Then play this course, set just 35 miles north of the California state line near the Rogue River. You see volcanoes all around, but are playing in a gently rolling valley, with some impressive water to play around, too.

- Address: 100 Eagle Point Drive, Eagle Point, OR 97524
- Phone: 541-826-8225
- Yardage: 7099
- Par: 72
- Rating: 74.3
- Slope: 131
- Greens Fee: $40-$48

Far West

1. Rio Secco Golf Club, Henderson, Nevada

This course is part of the Rio Suite Hotel and Casino, and it's not far from the Las Vegas Strip. Play here first, before you lose your money at the tables. The setting is a dramatic canyon, the Black Mountains loom in the background, and the fairways are lined with abundant stratified rock, boulders, and desert scrub. Stay on the grass if you can.

- Address: 2851 Grand Hills Drive, Henderson, NV 89052
- Phone: 888-396-2483 or 702-252-7777
- Yardage: 7332
- Par: 72
- Rating: 75.7
- Slope: 142
- Greens Fee: $190

2. The Resort at Squaw Creek, Squaw Valley, California

Site of the 1960 Olympics, Squaw Valley remains a world-class ski center. But, if you'd looked at this narrow valley, through which you must pass on the way to the ski hill, before the resort hotel and golf course were built, you'd have simply said "no way!" Well, they got it in here, and you'd better be able to hit the ball straight. Fairways are narrow, landing areas and greens are small, and wetlands are everywhere. But it's beautiful, and a small sampling of holes moves up the hillside to give a mountain course feel. This is an Audubon International Certified Cooperative Sanctuary, maintained without chemical pesticides. Kudos to them for that.

- Address: 400 Squaw Creek Road, Olympic Valley, CA 96146
- Phone: 800-403-4434 or 530-583-6300
- Web site: *www.squawcreek.com*
- Yardage: 6931
- Par: 71
- Rating: 72.9
- Slope: 140
- Greens Fee: $115

3. Aviara Golf Club, Carlsbad, California

Well, you've got to do something if you're in San Diego besides wait down by the Navy yards for the fleet to come in. This is one of the area's best courses. It reaches more than 7,000 feet but features huge greens, and it climbs and descends significant hills to add to the fun. They've been building like crazy here in recent years, but it's still a fine place to play.

- Address: 7447 Batiquitos Drive, Carlsbad, CA 92009
- Phone: 760-603-6900
- Yardage: 7007
- Par: 72
- Rating: 74.2
- Slope: 137
- Greens Fee: $175

Section VI
Computers and Technology

The 6 Best Computer Golf Games and Simulators

I will be the first to admit it: There are some thing I don't get. Fantasy leagues are one of them; computer games that purport to simulate the real thing are another. Clearly I am in the minority here, as evidenced by the popularity of both phenomena. So, without further complaints, and for those who must, here is a list of the best electronic golf games and simulations. Really, when you think about it, why not play these games? It beats actually having to get out there and practice your swing.

1. Jack Nicklaus 5!

This is probably the most popular of the computer games. You get 3-D effects, you can play on hundreds of actual courses, and the maker's commitment to realism is obvious. Fore!

- Producer: Accolade
- Info at: 800-245-7744
- List Price: $40
- You'll probably pay: $19.95
- Requires: Pentium-120, 16MB RAM, 30MB disk space, SVGA, 4X CD-ROM drive, Windows 95; Sound Blaster or compatible sound card

2. Tiger Woods PGA Tour 2001

In this one, not only can you play courses, but you can *be* golfers. The Golf Links 2001 Course Disk really does provide accurate and realistic re-creations of championship courses. You can pretend to be Tiger, of course; or, if you'd rather see what it's like to be chasing the Tiger, you can be Justin Leonard, Mark O'Meara, Stuart Appleby, Jim Furyk, or Steve Stricker. There are other features, too, like competing in simulated tournaments, team play, and even a driving range so you can practice your shots (but shouldn't you be at the real driving range?).

- Producer: EA Sports
- Info at: 800-245-4525; *www.ea.com*
- List Price: $40
- You'll probably pay: $39.95
- Requires: Pentium II-266, 64MB RAM, 4X CD-ROM

3. Links LS 2000

Links LS 2000 is the newest edition of the best-selling golf simulation game. These guys even have their own Tour: the VGA (Virtual Golf Association) Tour. In the year 2000, the VGA Tour staged its championship in Hawaii and awarded a $100,000 first prize. (Hey, maybe we all should forget about playing the real thing.) The game also won the 2000 Codie Award at the InfoSoft Summit in San Diego from the Software and Information Industry Association (SIIA) as Best Sports Game of Year. The game features championship courses, crowds cheering just for *you*, leader boards, grandstands, a dozen different golfers to pretend to be, and television-style commentary. "Links Lessons" even teaches you the fundamentals of electronic play. You know what? This is scary. You could lose your touch with reality here.

- Producer: Access/Microsoft
- Info at: 425-882-8080; *www.microsoft.com/catalog*
- List Price: $55
- You'll probably pay: $35 to $45
- Requires: Pentium-200, Windows 95/98/NT with Service Pack 3, 32MB RAM, 450MB disk space, 4X CD-ROM drive, 1MB video card, 32-bit sound card, 28.8K modem for online play

4. Links Extreme

Now, this *isn't* real. It seems to combine traditional computer game violence and fantasy with the idea of playing golf. Here, you encounter exploding golf balls, wandering zombies, and a demolition driving range, all while animatronic cows, flamingos, and deer stroll across the range. "Blast snooty golfers in plaid pants," says the promo material. Now you're talking!

- Producer: Microsoft
- Info at: 425-882-8080; *www.microsoft.com/catalog*
- List Price: $30
- You'll probably pay: $30
- Requires: Pentium-166 MMX, 32MB RAM, 60MB disk space, 1MB video card. Recommended: Pentium-200, 64MB RAM

5. Beavis and Butt-Head: Bunghole-in-one

More Gen-X phantasmagorical golf fun. Here you get to handle nacho cheese lava flows, lava lamps, tombstones, and buzz saws, as you "explore the demented world of Beavis and Butt-head." Fun and funny.

- Producer: GT Interactive
- Info at: 425-398-3074; *www.infogrames.com*
- List Price: $19.95
- You'll probably pay: $9.99
- Requires: Pentium-133, 16 MB RAM, 4X CD-ROM, 2MB video card, mouse, Windows 95. Recommended: Pentium-200, 32MB RAM, 4X CD-ROM, 4MB video card

6. The Golf Pro Classic

You only get two courses here—St. Mellion and Hilton Head—but realism is what this game is after. It also features television-style commentary, fully featured practice rounds, and even lessons from Gary Player. Go ahead, play through.

- Producer: Empire Interactive
- Info at: 415-439-4859; *www.empireinteractive.com/us*
- List Price: $19.95
- You'll probably pay: $11.95
- Requires: Pentium-90, 16 MB RAM, 4X CD-ROM, SVGA w/ 1MB, mouse, sound board, Windows 95. Recommended: Pentium 133, 32MB RAM, 270MB free hard drive space, 12x CD-ROM

Top 10 Golf Web Sites

Web sites come and go more fleetingly than the flutters of a pre-teen-aged girl's heart. However, here are the cremè-de-la-cremè of what I found as I surfed…and surfed…and surfed.

1. *Golfonline.com*

The Web site of *Golf Magazine*, it's probably the best all-around site online. The top course rankings are great, and the ability to link to find information on nearly any course in the world is nifty.

2. *Golf.com*

This site offers links to all the tours, feature articles…the whole nine yards. It has sections that include architecture, business, classified ads, commentary, equipment, golf for women, instruction, kids' golf, readers' forum, real estate, regional, tee time reservations, travel, and courses.

3. *Bunkershot.com*

This Web site describes itself as "a grassroots site for golfers from around the world." In addition to good articles, shopping, and even a chance to write your own articles, it has a good golf search function.

4. *Golfeurope.com*

Why bother here in America with a European golf site? Well, isolationism hasn't been chic since the Depression. But, more importantly, this is a great resource. You'll not only get an extensive guide to European courses and country clubs, but instruction, history, rules, biographies of the great golfers, trivia, a review of the rules, and a whole bunch more.

4. Duffers Golf Association (*duffersonline.com*)

This is a wonderful site for the less-than-perfect, beginner, or ace golfer with a sense of humor. You get a lot of history, an appreciation for why golfers play the game, a money winners list, instruction, online games, shopping, and a special section for females. I appreciate sites that are a bit self-deprecating and understand the fact that most of us are unworthy of caddying Arnie's trips to the junkyard and will never perfect this game.

5. The Golf Course (*library.thinkquest.org/10556*)

This high-tech golf Web site offers insight into the history of golf and a golf trivia game. You'll find humor, a section for teachers, the opportunity to read the site in four languages, and information on psychology, history, equipment, and more.

6. The Lady Golfer or Women's Golf (*womensgolf.about.com/sports/womensgolf*)

The original Web site joined the *About.com* family, which does an excellent job of covering specific subjects through the leadership of "local guides," people who are experts on their subject area. This site has it all—instruction, advice, articles, profiles, and chat—from a female player's perspective.

7. *Golflink.com*

This complete site offers an excellent collection for links to courses throughout the United States. Looking for places to play in Alaska? Just click on the map, then link directly to the course of your choice. Of course, there's shopping, tips, and all that stuff, plus golf/travel features, which offer fine reading.

8. Top 100 Golf Sites (*www.visittop100.com/golfsites*)

This Web site ranks, from 1 to 100, the best golf sites as voted by people who use them. You, too, can vote and influence the rankings. Or, better still, you can link to the sites on there and maybe improve your state of mind, if not your game. Golf sites are ranked by popularity, the stats are updated every 10 minutes, and the list is reset weekly.

9. *GolfHelp.com*

A veritable treasure trove of links for linksters, this site will lead you to information on just about anything and everything—including, for Pete's sake, where to find golf clip art, betting sites, and foreign language sites. Link on!

10. About.com Golf (*golf.about.com/sports/golf/mbody.htm*)

About.com is about everything, and in this case, golf. There's chat, opinion, reviews, and links to all manner of golf topics. This is a good general starting point when looking for stuff.

31 Top 10 Web Sites for Equipment

I t's hard to imagine that you can actually buy *custom-fitted* golf clubs on line, but you can. You can also buy just about anything else golf related on the Web these days. Although there's a chance that some of these sites may have disappeared into the void, they were all good when I tested them.

1. *Golfballs.com*

Here is everything—and I mean *everything*—in golf balls: new, used, bulk, illegal, floaters, range, trick balls, balls for night play, and logo over-runs. Such a deal!

2. *Findgolfstuff.com*

This is a cyberspace discount department store of golf. It features departments including accessories, apparel, bags, books/videos, clubs, gifts, health/fitness, jewelry, software, training, and travel. You'll find everything from big name clubs to goo for shining your old clubs. Used clubs and balls, more gadgets than you can shake a stick at, and even help selling your old clubs are available here.

3. Yahoo Shopping (*www.yahoo.com*)

This major search engine puts you in touch with more than 2,000 equipment listings: stores, online stores, guys who operate out of their basements, guys who operate out of *your* basement. Is this the ultimate shopping mall for golf junk? Probably.

4. The Golf Equipment Club (*www.golfequipmentclub.com*)

This free-membership golf club provides golf equipment, including custom club fitting for any club. I like the "Ask Dr. Golf" column and a "mall" to link to myriad other products from flowers to whatever. The prices aren't bad, either, and there's free shipping in the continental United States.

5. Wholesale Golf Equipment (*www.wholesalegolfequipment.com*)

Now here's a site that not only offers all the major brands at off-prices, but displays its own Hall of Fame, plus salient (not necessarily relevant) quotes from Abraham Lincoln, Teddy Roosevelt, and John F. Kennedy. The prices are good, shipping costs are reasonable, and the range of offerings is certainly wide enough to keep most equipment junkies happy. The site itself is beset with some overkill in the way of initial graphics, which can slow you down to the point where you might look elsewhere.

6. *Golfmonster.com*

Yes, it lives up to its name. Truly a monster, this site lets you choose from among the following categories: clubs, bags, balls, shoes, gloves, apparel, accessories, art, memorabilia, teaching aids, books, videos, software, team merchandise, home/gift, and closeouts. You can search by manufacturer or category.

7. *GigAgolf.com*

These guys specialize in selling their own version of the big names' clubs for a fraction of the price. They do it by creating clubs using top brand components—heads, shafts, and grips—and eschewing the need to pay pros to play with and hype their gear. You can fully customize these clubs, and they get shipped pronto with a money-back guarantee. They feature a closeout and weekly specials section. They sell some gadgets and bags also, but clubs are the big deal here.

8. *GolfCircuit.com*

A shop out of San Diego, GolfCircuit.com offers competitive prices on equipment, travel, and more. The site has a nice feel, and it even offers a rules-of-golf-made-easy link, in case you want to find out if you've been cheating (you already know the answer, but go ahead—double check).

9. *Laksengolf.com*

Here is another California shop gone online. This one comes with a "tip of the month." The range of companies offered isn't that great, but you get the feeling that the companies it does handle it knows inside and out.

10. *Golfoutlet.com*

Here is a veritable supermarket of golf stuff. You don't get the personalized feel or service of some of the other sites, but you get good product range and pricing, plus golf course reviews, videos, books, and more.

Top 10 Web Sites for Travel Information

Y ou can travel the world without leaving your desk via the wonders of modern electronic communication.

1. Golf and Travel (*www.golfandtravel.com*)

This beautiful site features magnificent photos and elaborate information for the places it covers, divided by types of destinations: mountains, islands, international, the Southwest, and so on. It's very high-end and was still in development at press time, but it looked like a very worthwhile site to visit.

2. Kabash (*www.kabash.com/activitytravel/golf.htm*)

Kabash is a travel search engine, and from here you get descriptions of and links to a number of golf travel sites, including some in this list.

3. *Thegolfdeal.com*

Thegolfdeal.com presents a five-step process in which you answer questions about where you want to go, what courses you want play, when, and how long you want to be there. Then the site comes up with a retail price for the trip, after which you can make an offer and even barter. Makes you feel like a wheeler-dealer.

4. Golf Destinations (*www.golfpac.com*)

Here is a place to research golf vacation prices, from packages to guided tours and online tee times.

5. *Travelscape.com*

This site attempts to be full service, with lots of options, featured deals, and package deals. It offers a destination guide and a featured destination, and lots of content, although it is somewhat cumbersome to use. The online tee time page is nice, and the extensive reservations section appears to work well.

6. *Byebyenow.com*

With a wide array of golf vacation packages (61 at press time), *Byebyenow.com* functions as an online travel agent. It is particularly good for folks who are after vacation packages.

7. Player's Choice (*Playerschoicegolf.com*)

This is a good international site where you can search by location, featured destination, or special deals.

8. Posh Golf (*www.posh-golf-travel.com*)

The vacation spots on this British site were amassed by former *Golf Monthly* travel editor Barry Ward from more than 400 golf resorts he has personally visited. It covers the Caribbean, Europe, the Mediterranean, Africa, Asia, and the United States. You determine costs by linking to a recommended golf tour operator.

9. Wide World of Golf (*www.wideworldofgolf.com*)

This is a high-end tour operator that specializes in guided tours and cruises to pretty exotic places. It goes to Japan, Scotland, Ireland, and Africa on various golf cruises, and even offers an Around-the-World Tour. Check out the French Canal Barge Tour, or the Asia Golf and Shopping Spree.

10. The Golf Circuit (*www.golfcircuit.com/travel*)

This is a good, solid site for the basics of planning a golf vacation in the United States. Hundreds of golf resorts and hotels are listed in great detail, and there are plentiful discounts for families and non-golfers.

33

Top 10 Web Sites for Course Information

Choosing places to play has always befuddled me. How can anyone tell what a course is like from reading descriptions or even looking a photos? Go out and play it; if it's great or it stinks, you'll soon find out. Still, folks want to preview their options, and there seems to be no limit to the number of Web sites that will feed you information. It's up to you, however, to make the information useful in some way.

1. *Golflink.com*

This is a complete site with an excellent collection for links to courses throughout the United States and a direct hook-up to *golfcourse.com* (see Chapter 29).

2. Top 100 Golf Sites (*www.visittop100.com/golfsites*)

This site ranks, from 1 to 100, the best golf sites as voted by people who use them (see Chapter 29).

3. *Golfcourse.com*

Part of *Golfonline.com* (see Chapter 29), this site provides comprehensive information on more than 20,000 courses worldwide, divided by country, region, state or province, and so on.

4. USA Golf Greens (*www.usagolfgreens.com*)

This comprehensive nationwide golf course directory lets you whittle things down by state, then region, then course. The presentation is strictly statistical, but it gives you all the basic information you'll ever need. Not too much in the way of evaluation, though, if other people's opinions matter to you.

5. Golf Public (*www.golfpublic.com*)

Golf Public ranks public golf courses and golf resorts. Included are hundreds of links to golf vacations, destinations, schools, businesses, and other golf-related links. The actual reviews of public courses are limited, but there are dozens of links to courses in and outside the United States.

6. Best Courses to Play (*www.bestcoursestoplay.com*)

This state-by-state listing of recommended courses offers a few links, but for the most part, if you see a course that catches your eye, you'll have to look elsewhere to find specific information on it. But if you only want to know if this site thinks a particular course is worthwhile, it's worth a look.

7. *Golfersweb.com*

America's public golf courses are divided by region. You select a region to find a course, then link to the rankings page, where the courses are graded in thwo categories: affordable (under $50) and upscale (over $50). This site offers detail, evaluation, and even a layout map for each course.

8. *Golfhelp.com*

This very good golf search engine leads you to dozens of sites that will tell you about courses.

9. Golf Caddie (*www.golfcaddie.com*)

Golfcaddie.com claims to provide comprehensive information about more than 16,000 golf courses, including nearby hotels and other travel services. It attempts to be a one-stop shop where you can enter a location and your personal desires for course criteria, and get a list of nearby courses, hotels, and so forth. You should even find course policies, greens fees, and guest policies.

10. *Golfonline.com*

This is the online version of *Golf Magazine*, done in conjunction with ESPN (see Chapter 16). It lists the top 100 you can play, as well as top courses by region. It has a terrific course search engine and can help you make travel arrangements.

34

6 Web Sites for Golf Gifts and Gadgets

Because good gadgets and potentially bogus ones were listed in Chapter 12, it only seems fair to give you the latest electronic resources for finding such gizmos and contraptions. You can imagine how many options there are, and how much they vary in quality, reliability, and plain old usefulness.

1. *GolfGadgets.com*

You'd have to go with a site that used this as its name, wouldn't you? A function of the V-Que Company of Newport Beach, California, this site has all kinds of stuff: videos, swing trainers, headcovers, and even a kids' training video. There are gifts, too, of course. I like the portable, adjustable putting cup for only $8.

2. *Technogadgets.com*

This is not a golf site, but rather an electronics gizmo site. Still, if it's electronic and it relates to golf, you'll probably find it here. Perfect for your golf-playing computer geek. Among the noteworthy gadgets found here: an automatic handicapper, an electronic putting challenge that offers 72 different contours on which to putt, Lectronickaddy (a remote-controlled caddy that carries your clubs), a cordless blender for your golf cart, a lightning detector, and GolfGuide (a handheld device that stores information on more than 13,000 U.S. golf courses). Who could ask for more?

3. *Golfx.com*

This is not a comprehensive assortment of gadgets, but a fascinating, creative, and useful collection that's entertaining, too.

4. *Findgolfstuff.com*

This site offers one of the most complete inventories of googles, gimmicks, and doohickeys online (see Chapter 29).

5. *Wheatroadgolf.com*

A function of Wheat Road Golf of Vineland, New Jersey, its list of accessories is long and impressive. It also does a good job on regular equipment, too.

6. *Chipshot.com*

The accessories department even has gizmos for your electric cart, novelty head covers, and golf toilet paper.

Top 10 Computer Golf Programs

Face it, we live in the computer age. There's a computer program to track just about everything in life, and golf is no exception. Here is a variety of choices that perform a variety of functions. None of these are necessary to daily survival but, then again, neither is watching the Masters on television. You do it because it's fun. Just remember, all the statistical programs require that *somebody* does the data entry.

1. Pebble Beach Golf Links Multi-Media Course Guide

This is a very specific program; it covers only Pebble Beach. Johnny Miller takes you on an interactive, hole-by-hole tour of the course, tossing in tips, instruction, and personal anecdotes. It's the perfect program for the guy who dreams of playing Pebble Beach but probably will never get there, or for the guy who finally is going to get there just once and wants to be more than fully prepared.

- Producer: Golf Media, Inc.
- Info at: *www.golfmedia.com*
- List Price: $24.95
- Requires: Microsoft Windows 95 or 3.1, 486/66 DX-2 CPU, 8MB RAM, 8-bit VGA display or higher, 2X CD-Rom drive, Windows-compatible sound device, mouse

2. National Golf Course Directory

The maker claims to include every golf course in the United States: public, private, military, and resort, more than 14,000 in all. You can search by state, city, zip code, or even slope rating, and get the full scoop on your PC or laptop.

- Producer: SportsWare Technologies
- Info at: 800-357-2202; *www.play18.com*
- Price: $14.95
- Requires: 386/33 Mhz or faster processor, 4 MB RAM, Windows 3.1

3. Handicap Manager for Windows

This is one of several programs that tracks scores, calculates handicaps, and spews back a variety of statistics. You can store up to 255 rounds and monitor the handicaps of 800 of your closest friends.

- Producer: Northern Systems, Inc.
- Info at: 613-825-9691; *www.northernsystems.com*
- Price: $34.95
- Requires: Windows 95, 33 Mhz processor, 8 MB RAM, 2 MB hard disk space

4. The Golfer's Diary CD-Rom

Here is another statistics chaser that can keep an eye on your performance trends, give you reviews of each of your rounds, and remind you of what you did and how you fared at the driving range, while also providing course information and scorecards.

- Producer: TQ Personal Sports Software, Inc.
- Info at: 905-634-6110; *www.tqs.net*
- Price: $24.95
- Requires: Windows 95

5. Ultra-Caddie for Palm Pilots

This is an electronic caddie that fits in your pocket. It will coach you in such esoterica as club selection, track your shot accuracy, and such must-know items as greens in regulation, birdies, pars, bogies, net score, and adjusted score. How did we ever survive without this when all we had was a scorecard and pencil? It also does the "accounting" for most popular side games and provides up-to-the-minute status of the games in progress, including "what if" scenarios. And last but not least, it offers a RoundAnalyzer function for your PC so you'll really know how bad you are!

- Producer: 3 Wedge/SportSoft Golf
- Info at: *www.ultracaddie.com*
- Price: $59.95
- Requires: Palm Pilot. Or, for computer: Windows 95, video capable of 256 colors at 800x600 resolution, 25MB hard disk, 150 mhz, 32MB RAM

6. Golf Clubmaking Software

For do-it-yourselfers, this may be the ultimate club-planning and building software. You can custom fit golf clubs from components, using your computer to simulate head, shaft, and grip combinations and customize swing weight and perfectly match it to head weight, shaft weight, grip weight, club length or shaft length using the program's "What If" feature. The maker includes golf club assembly plans and tells you how to get free component catalogs, how to choose components, and how and where to buy the tools you need. Because I've never built anything that worked, this is all a mystery to me. But, if you're a Mr. or Ms. Fix-It kind of person, this just may be what you're looking for.

- Producer: Golf Perfect Software
- Info at: *www.golfperfect.com*
- Price: $19.95
- Requires: Windows 3.1, 95, 98 compatible. 486SX, 486DX, or any Pentium PC compatible

7. Handicalc Plus Golf Software

This program handles handicapping for groups from 25 to 200 golfers. Best if you bring along 199 of your closest friends! You can track scores, birdies, pars, bogeys, greens in regulation, fairways hit, and just about any other trivial statistic you are compelled to pursue. The maker says it will let you "learn exactly where you are losing strokes and make those improvements necessary to lower your score!" I *know* where I'm losing strokes—on nearly every shot. But, if your game is more evolved than mine, this kind of tracking just may help you move to the next level.

- Producer: ABACUS International Corporation
- Info at: 800-932-8208 or 206-935-8200; *www.handicalc.com*
- Price: $29
- Requires: Windows 95

9. GolfMaster/2000

Want to calculate statistics for up to 999 golfers? Plan a trip for 32? Track information for up to 999 courses? Set up pairings and schedule playing groups and tee times? Track your own personal Skins Game or your group's ongoing cumulative results? This program will do that for you. It will not cook your breakfast.

- Producer: Focus 2000
- Info at: 800-937-7717; *www.focus2k.com/golfmast.htm*
- Price: $79.50
- Requires: Windows 95/98/NT/2000/ME Operating Systems, 32-bit Pentium or equivalent processor

10. Mulligan's Golf Personal

This is the only program designed specifically for the Macintosh Operating System. It does all the stuff the others do, but it'll do it on your Apple product. But somebody *still* has to enter all the data.

- Producer: Mulligans' Software
- Info at: 972-407-9306; *www.mulligansw.com*
- Price: $39.95
- Requires: 68020+ Macintosh, PowerMac or iMac running System 7 or later, including MacOS 8 and 9

Section VII
Miscellaneous

10 Great Golf Jokes

1. Slow Golf

Two men were having an awfully slow round of golf because the two women in front of them managed to get into every sand trap, lake, and rough on the course. They didn't bother to wave the men on through, which is, naturally, proper golf etiquette.

After two hours of waiting and waiting, one of the men said, "I think I'll walk up there and ask those gals to let us play through."

He walked out to the fairway, got halfway to the ladies, stopped, turned around, and came back. "I can't do it," he said. "One of those women is my wife and the other is my mistress! Maybe you'd better go talk to them."

The second man walked toward the ladies, got halfway there and, just as his partner had done, stopped, turned around, and walked back. "Small world," he said.

2. The Difference Between Golf and Tennis

The difference between golf and tennis is that tennis is murder—you just want to kill the other player. Golf is suicide—you just want to kill yourself...

3. Heaven and Earth

Near the end of a particularly trying round of golf, during which the golfer had hit numerous fat shots, he said in frustration to his caddy, "I'd move heaven and earth to break a hundred on this course."

"Try heaven," said the caddy. "You've already moved most of the earth."

4. Drowning Man

A hack golfer spends a day at a plush country club, playing golf and enjoying the luxury of a complimentary caddy. Being a hack golfer, of course, he plays poorly all day.

Round about the 18th hole, he spots a lake off to the left of the fairway. He looks at the caddy and says, "I've played so poorly all day, I think I'm going to go drown myself in that lake."

The caddy looks at the lake. The caddy looks back at the golfer. "I don't think you could keep your head down that long," he says.

5. It's a Gimme

It was on the first tee where Sally and Harry met for the first time. They decided to play a round together because their usual playing partners were no-shows. Each told the other that he and she was a hacker. And that is the way it was on the first two holes. But on the third hole, which was a par-five, they both hit pro-like drives. Both claimed they had never hit a shot like that before. Similar remarks followed their second shots, each of which appeared to have rolled on the green.

They did indeed find both balls on the green. Harry's ball was away at about 30 feet from the hole.

As Harry was lining up his putt he said, "I've never even made a par on this hole before. If I sink this putt for an eagle, I'll be too excited to go on with this round. What do you say we just go have a few drinks and a fancy lunch to celebrate my eagle if I make it?"

Sally agreed and Harry made his eagle putt.

After Harry settled down a bit, Sally looked over her eagle putt from about 20 feet. She told Harry that she'd never carded less than a double bogie on the hole.

"So," she said, "if I make this putt, let's buy a bottle, skip the lunch, get a motel room, and celebrate in bed for the rest of the day!"

To which Harry said, "Honey, pick up your ball. That's a gimme if I ever saw one!"

6. New Clubs

"I just got a new set of golf clubs for my husband," says the wife to her friend.

"Gee, what a great trade," replies the friend.

7. 4-Wood and a Putt

Standing on the tee of a relatively long par three, the confident golfer said to his caddy, "Looks like a 4-wood and a putt to me." The caddy handed him the 4-wood, which he topped about 15 yards off the front of the tee.

Immediately the caddy handed him his putter and said, "And now for one hell of a putt."

8. Idiots

Two long-time golfers were standing at the third tee overlooking the river.

One golfer looked to the other and said, "Look at those idiots fishin' in the rain."

9. Golf Psalm

The pro is my shepherd,
I shall not slice.
He maketh me to drive straight
down green fairways;
He leadeth me safely
across still water hazards;
He restoreth my approach shots
He leadeth me in the paths of
accuracy for my game's sake.
Yea, though I chip through the
shadows of sand traps,

I will fear no bogies.

For his advice is with me;

His putter and irons,

they comfort me.

He prepareth my strategy for me

in the presence of mine opponents;

He anointeth my head with confidence:

The cup will not be runneth over!

Surely birdies and eagles shall follow

me all the rounds of my life,

And I will score in the low 80s—forever.

10. Headaches

Joe was a moderately successful golfer, but as he got older he was increasingly hampered by incredible headaches. His golf, personal hygiene, and love life started to suffer. He managed to push on, but when his game turned really sour he sought medical help. After being referred from one specialist to another, he finally came across a doctor who offered a solution.

"The good news is I can cure your headaches," said the physician. "The bad news is that it will require castration. You have a very rare condition that causes your testicles to press up against the base of your spine. The pressure creates one hell of a headache. The only way to relieve the pressure and allow your swing to work again is to remove the testicles."

Joe was shocked and depressed. He wondered if he had anything to live for, but then figured at least he could play reasonable golf again. He decided he had no choice but to go under the knife. When he left the hospital, his mind was clear, but he felt like he was missing an important part of himself. As he walked down the street, he realized that he felt like a different person. He could make a new beginning, swing free, and live a new life. He went to the club for a drink and as he walked past the pro shop he thought, "That's what I need: a new outfit."

He entered the shop and told the salesman, "I'd like some new golf slacks." The salesman eyed him briefly and said, "Let's see...size 44 long."

Joe laughed, "That's right, how did you know?"

"It's my job."

Joe tried on the slacks, and they fit perfectly.

As Joe admired himself in the mirror, the salesman asked, "How about a new shirt? I've got some great new Nicklaus in stock."

Joe thought for a moment and then said, "Sure."

The salesman eyed Joe and said, "Let's see...34 sleeve and...16 and a half neck"

Joe was surprised and said, "That's right, how did you know?"

"It's my job."

Joe tried on the shirt, and it fit perfectly.

As Joe adjusted the collar in the mirror, the salesman asked, "How about new shoes? We got new soft spikes in just the other day." Joe was on a roll and agreed. The salesman said, "Let's see...9 and a half...wide."

Joe was astonished, "That's right, how did you know?"

"It's my job."

Joe tried on the shoes and they fit perfectly.

Joe walked comfortably around the shop and the salesman asked, "How about a new hat?" Without hesitating, Joe said, "Sure."

The salesman eyed Joe's head and said, "Let's see...7 and five-eighths."

Joe was really impressed, "That's right, how did you know?"

"It's my job."

The hat fit perfectly. Joe was feeling really great now, and the salesman asked, "How about some new underwear? We've got some great new imported stuff." Joe thought for a second and said, "Sure."

The salesman stepped back, eyed Joe's waist, and said, "Let's see...size 36."

Joe laughed, "No, I've worn size 34 since I was 18 years old."

The salesman shook his head sadly, "You can't wear a size 34. Every time you swing it would press your testicles up against the base of your spine and give you one hell of a headache."

37

10 Reasons Golf Is Better Than Sex

1. You always know when the end is in sight. And, if you want to go another round, there's no need for a recovery period.

2. Pace is generally even throughout the match. And, even if you start slowly, you don't have to quicken the pace at the finish.

3. Size never matters. Just skill and sensitivity.

4. It's easier to take criticism for bad putts than criticism about your putz.

5. "Golf," it has been said, "is the most fun you can have with your clothes on." And besides, you can hide reality underneath those clothes if you need to.

6. "Golf is 90 percent inspiration and 10 percent perspiration," according to Johnny Miller. Sex, it seems, might qualify as the other way around.

7. In golf, it's much easier to score. Or, as Jack Lemmon has said: "If you think it's hard to meet new people, try picking up the wrong golf ball."

8. Shaft stiffness can be varied, and sometimes less stiff brings better results.

9. You can start each day with brand new balls.

10. The afterglow not only lasts longer, but you've got a written record of your success.

38

5 Worst Shots Ever Hit in PGA Tournament Play

I t *is* comforting to realize that even the best of the best sometimes do the things that we duffers do: top shots that roll only a few feet; bugger chips that roll across the green and down the hill, to be followed by an equally bad blast that returns the player to whence he just came; or shots that bounce off things and turn the golf game momentarily into something resembling bumper pool. The stories are legion, of course. Here are five select tournament play shots that wreaked havoc with the golfer who'd hit them but which, frankly, make us feel a lot better about things.

1. Doug Sanders: 1970

Doug Sanders won a few tournaments in his time. Nineteen of them to be exact. But it was a 4-foot putt for victory in the 1970 British Open that lays claim to his fame. He'd never won a Major, you see, and had even had to pre-qualify just to get into the tournament. No pre-qualifier had ever won it, and here was this 4-foot putt that could provide two firsts. A simple four-footer. He blew it, then lost to Nicklaus by a stroke in the playoff.

2. Greg Norman: 1996

Well, this isn't really just a shot. It's a whole round of shots that add up to one of the worst turnarounds in Major competition history. Norman led the Masters by six shots going into the final round. He was coming off a course record 63 for

Round One. But not only did he blow it with a six-over final round, he was four over for the back nine alone; his round was built from five bogeys and two double-bogeys. All on television—for all the world to see.

3. Seve Ballesteros: 1979

Sometimes disaster doesn't spell defeat. Ballesteros long had a reputation for Steve-Martinesque wild-and-crazy play. Massively errant shots followed by miraculous recoveries were his stock in trade, especially in his younger days. But, on the 16th hole during the 1979 British Open final round—a day on which he had hit few fairways off the tee anyway—he sent his drive into a parking lot at a point where he held the lead over Jack Nicklaus by a mere two strokes. Oddly, the parking lot was not out of bounds. Seve was entitled to a free drop, saved the hole with a miracle wedge shot, and went on to win by three, the first Spaniard ever to do so. Perhaps we should all be aiming for the parking lot with our driver.

4. Johnny Miller: 1973

Before he was a big star on the Tour, Miller found himself in position to win the 1973 Atlanta Open. All that was required was a par five on the 18th. The hole itself was not particularly challenging. But even future champions seize up with nerves, and Miller whacked only a so-so drive. As the ball headed towards the first cut of rough, a problem became apparent. There was a woman sitting on a metal folding chair—right in the line of fire. The woman jumped up, avoiding a calamitous encounter with the flying sphere. Alas, she left the chair in place. Incredibly, the ball hit the chair at just the right angle of incidence and velocity to carom high into the air and sharply to the right. It landed just a few inches out of bounds. Penalties had to be assessed. Miller victories would have to wait.

5. Harry Bradshaw: 1949

Okay, so maybe Harry Bradshaw, unlike Terry Bradshaw, is not a household name these days, but in the 1940s this Bradshaw was a well-respected if slightly over-the-hill pro who prided himself on his sense of honor. This incident took place at the British Open, played that year at Sandwich. It was on the fifth hole in the final round. The man hit his drive well into the rough and found his ball comfortably huddled in the bottom half of a broken beer bottle.

Now, of course, the rules state that this would likely qualify as an unplayable lie. But Mr. Bradshaw eschewed a ruling, choosing to play on rather than wait for someone to trudge out from the clubhouse and decide what was proper. In his mind, if you play into a beer bottle, you play out of it. So he smashed the vessel/ball combination with his wedge, splaying broken glass in all directions, but only moving the ball a piddling 25 yards or so. Perhaps it was the flying glass that unnerved him but, whatever the cause, he took a double-bogey six on the hole and went on to tie for the championship, which he consequently lost in a playoff. The moral here, perhaps, is never hit the bottle when you can take a drop.

5 Most Memorable Shots in PGA Tournament History

1. Francis Ouimet: 1913

The year is 1913; the site is the U.S. Open at The Country Club in Brookline, Massachusetts. Golf in America remains largely a British game, played in the States only by stuffy, upper-crust Yanks. Tournaments are dominated by Brits, until Francis Ouimet signs up to play in the Open. Who is Ouimet? He's a 20-year-old caddie. After the 36-hole qualifying rounds, the famed Brits Ted Ray and Harry Vardon lead with 148 and 151, respectively. This guy Ouimet sits at 152. Come the final day, all three are tied at 225. They play in the rain. Vardon and Ray shoot a meager 79, but under the conditions, not bad. Ouimet is out at 43, then bloats a five on the 10th. By the time he reaches 17, he needs a birdie to tie—and these are two tough holes. He leaves himself a 20-footer for the birdie, a downhill, angled putt. With little fuss, he holes it, pars 18 easily to tie the two big-wigs, and goes on to win the ensuing playoff by five strokes over Vardon and six over Ray. The story plays on newspaper front pages nationwide, and suddenly golf becomes an American game. Said Ouimet years later, "That one putt did it."

2. Gene Sarazen's Double-Eagle: 1935

The 15th at Augusta National played in 1925 at 485 yards, a par-five. By the time Gene Sarazen was getting ready to tee off there on the Masters final round, Craig Woods had birdied the 18th, apparently winning the tournament. Sarazen needed to play the final four holes in a four-under 12 if he was going to win it. His drive carried 250 yards. Rather than play up in front of the green-guarding water hazard, he smacked shot two with a 4-wood, not only clearing the water but, with the ball traveling some 235 yards, finding the green and the cup. A double-eagle two. He parred the final three and gained a tie. He won the 36-hole playoff by five. They call this one the "Shot Heard Round the World" because the newspaper coverage that followed took golf *and* Augusta National to new levels of popularity.

3. Ben Hogan: 1950

You have to love Ben Hogan. Nearly killed in a car crash, he came back to the top of the sport. At the 1950 U.S. Open, played at Merion Golf Club near Philadelphia, playing just a year and a half after the accident, Hogan showed the stuff of which he was made. Back then, they played 36 holes on the final day—particularly grueling for someone who had been as battered as Ben had been. He bogeyed 15 on the final round, and 17, too. He came to the 458-yard 18th needing a par four to tie. The drive was good. Hogan chose up a 2-iron for his third shot. The ball rolled to a stop just three feet from the cup. Hogan got his tie, and won the 18-hole playoff going away. Destiny's child, for sure.

4. Byron Nelson: 1939

Byron Nelson is a name synonymous with golf greatness. By 1939, he'd pretty much won it all, including 11 PGA tournaments in a row. Won it all, yes—except the U.S. Open. But, in 1939, he got some help. The great Sam Snead needed but a six on the final hole to tie

Byron Nelson, circa 1945

for the title, and he shot an incredible eight. That left three tied at the top: Nelson, Craig Wood, and Denny Shute. On 18 of the first playoff round, Nelson needed a 10-foot birdie putt to tie again, this time with Wood. The following playoff round saw Nelson take a one-stroke lead with a birdie at three. On the par-four fourth, after a good drive, Nelson took the hard road. He chose a 1-iron. He never saw where it went—just heard the crowd roar—until he arrived at the green. You know that old duffer's joke? The one that says, "If you can't find your ball anywhere else, look in the cup"? Nelson's was. He went on to win by three.

5. Arnold Palmer: 1960

Even if you were a flower child in the 1960s, you knew about Arnie and his army. It was in that first year of the decade that Palmer showed his signature stuff at the Masters. He needed two birdies in the final four holes to win. He parred numbers 15 and 16. He now needed birdies on two holes where, just the year before, he'd earned a pair of bogeys. He got the first one, then stood 120 yards off the green after his drive on 18. A 6-iron was his choice of weapon. He put it to within six feet of the pin. He got his birdie. He got his title. And he later was quoted as saying, "I don't think any single shot gave me a greater thrill, or was more important to me." Amen.

Top 5 U.S. Country Clubs for Gourmet Meals

For this list, I went to a higher authority. Larry Olmsted, editor and co-founder of *The Golf Insider* and food and wine columnist for *Luxury Golf Magazine* and *Investor's Business Daily*, has been forced to eat in high-end restaurants at golf resorts throughout the world. I felt so sorry for him that I thought he should have to give back to the "little people" (namely, us) by at least revealing where in the United States he's dined most notably. As with all the lists, only public access merits mention.

1. The American Club, Kohler, Wisconsin

A five-star resort with four world-class golf courses and a site of the U.S. Women's Open and, in a few years, of the PGA. The place houses some 14 or so restaurants, but it's The Immigrant that gets our expert's nod. The fine dining showcases the food of the major regions from which the Kohler people originate (yes, it's the bath fixtures folks who own this resort): Switzerland, Germany, and Central Europe. Also noteworthy is The Grill Room at Whistling Straits, which Olmsted calls "the best restaurant in any clubhouse."

2. The Broadmoor, Colorad Springs, Colorado

This is another five-star resort with multiple eateries. Here, our main man says, it doesn't matter where you eat. They're renowned for their western game (elk and caribou, for example), so bring your cowboy hat and chow down.

3. The Sagamore, Bolton Landing, New York

Among the restaurants at this longstanding upstate New York favorite, it's the fine dining room that gets the kudos. They feature a "wine pairing" menu every night that matches your order to fine wines (or, is it the other way around?). Olmstead says they have the best golf course hotel cocktail lounge food in the universe every afternoon with a raw bar spread, sushi, and authentic Spanish tapis menu.

4. Pebble Beach Resort, Pebble Beach, California

Pebble Beach pops up on another list. Olmsted thinks the golf (not to mention the *price* of the golf) gets so much attention that the cuisine is often overlooked. They've opened a branch of Roy's from Hawaii, featuring chef Roy Yamaguchi from The Food Channel, which is his first eatery on the mainland. Also noteworthy is Peppolli, a Tuscan restaurant owned by well-known Italian wine makers, the Antinori family.

5. Greg Norman's Australian Grill, Myrtle Beach, South Carolina

Nobody can accuse Myrtle Beach of being a high-cuisine capital (think all-you-can-eat buffets), but Greg Norman has opened this excellent restaurant with Todd English, the chef from Olive's. It's a Myrtle upscale highlight that can be found at the Barefoot Landing complex (site of four golf courses).

Trivia

Here's a list of random facts. At least I *think* they're facts. Well, I know that *I* didn't make them up.

- Arnold Palmer, in 1958, led the PGA Tour by winning $42,000.
- The tradition of yelling "fore" dates to the 18th century. Golfers then were often wealthy men who employed many personal servants. These gents would usually have a servant, or caddie, to carry their clubs and find their balls. Because courses were generally pretty rough and held many natural hazards, many players would make use of a forward caddie or "forecaddie"—somebody to scout ahead of the golfers and spot the ball where it landed. To alert the forecaddies that a shot was coming, the player would yell "fore!" and then swing away.
- Golf legend Laura Davies once won a long-driving competition by outhitting 40 men. Her winning shot measured 312 yards.
- A set of four clubs, a golf bag, and six balls cost $17.50 in 1922. Sold separately, they cost $20.50. The clubs included a driver or Brassie for $4; a Mashie for $3.50; a mid-iron for $3.50; a putter for $3.50; a bag for $3; and six balls for $3.

- The first recorded hole-in-one was achieved by Young Tom Morris during the 1868 British Open Championship at Preswick. Morris won four consecutive British Opens—a feat that has never been equaled.

- Jack Nicklaus earned his first pro pay check at the 1962 L.A. Open. He finished tied for 50th. He won $33.33.

- The first known round of golf on American soil was played on February 22, 1888, in a pasture adjacent to the home of one John Reid in Yonkers, New York. Reid and three others played a three-hole layout with just six clubs among them.

- The first U.S. Open in 1895 was an afterthought to the first U.S. Amateur. Played the day after the Amateur as a one-day, 36-hole event, it boasted a field of 11 contestants.

- The first British Open championship was held in 1860 at the Preswick club in Scotland. It had eight participants. Prize money was £10.

- Most expensive country club in the world: Koganei Country Club, Japan, where the membership fee is $2,344,000.

- The longest recorded hole-in-one: 447 yards by Robert Mitera of Omaha, Nebraska, on the 10th hole at the Miracle Hills Golf Club in Omaha.

- The longest recorded hole-in-one by a woman: 393 yards by Marie Robie of Wollaston, Massachusetts, on the first hole at Furnace Brook Golf Club in 1949.

- The most holes-in-one recorded in a single round: three by Dr. Joseph Boydstone of Bakersfield, California, on the third, fourth, and ninth holes at Bakersfield Country Club, October 10, 1962.

- The most consecutive birdies recorded in one round: 10 by pro John Irwin at St. Catherine's Golf and Country Club in 1984.

- World's longest golf course: The International Golf Club, Bolton, Massachusetts, 8,325 yards, par 77.

- World's longest par-seven: the sixth hole at Koolan Island Club in Western Australia, 948 yards.

- World's largest green: at the par-six, 695-yard, fifth at the International Golf Club in Bolton Massachusetts, 28,000 square feet.

- Largest recorded participation in a golf tournament: The Volkswagen Grand Prix Open Amateur Championship (UK)—321,778 competitors (206,820 men, 114,958 women).

- Francis Brown, golf addict, was tried and hanged in Banff, Scotland for stealing two golf balls in 1637.

- Fewest putts by a man in a single 18-hole round: 15 by pro Richard Stanwood in 1976 and amateur Ed Drysdale in 1985.

- Fewest putts by a woman in a single round: 17 by pro Joan Joyce.

- Most aces shot in a single year: 33 by Scott Palmer of San Diego, California, between June 5, 1983, and May 31, 1984.

- Lowest recorded score for 18 holes: 55 by Alfred Smith of England in 1936.

- Most consecutive PGA Tour wins: Byron Nelson with 11 in 1945.

- World's highest golf course: Tuctu Golf Club in Morococha, Peru, which stands at 14,335 feet above sea level at its lowest point.

- World's lowest golf course: Furnace Creek Golf Course in Death Valley, California.

- Oldest recorded playing foursome for cumulative age: 361 years, composed of Maurice Pease, age 98; Joseph Hooker, age 94; Richardson Bronson, age 85; and Stanley Hart Sr., age 84.

- Fastest round of golf ever played on foot: 28 minutes, 9 seconds by Gay Wright on the 6039-yard Tewantin-Noosa Golf Club in Queensland, Australia in 1980.

- The lowest recorded golf score for throwing a ball around 18 holes (more than 6,000 yards) is 82 by Joe Flynn, 21, at the 6,228-yard Port Royal Course in Bermuda on March 27, 1975.

- Floyd Satterlee Rood used the entire United States as a course, playing from the Pacific Ocean to the Atlantic Ocean between September 14, 1963, to October 3, 1964 in 114,737 strokes. He lost 3,511 balls on the 3,977-mile trail.
- Thad Daber, using only a 6-iron, played the 6,037-yard Lochmore Golf Course at Cary, North Carolina, in 73 on November 10, 1985, to win the World One-Club Championship.

Highest recorded scores:

- Chevalier von Cittern played 18 in 316, averaging 17.55 per hole, at Biarritz, France in 1888.
- Steven Ward required 222 strokes for the 6,212-yard, Pecos Course in Reeve County, Texas, on June 18, 1976, just under 4 years old!

Most shots for one hole:

- A player in the qualifying round of the 1912 Shawnee Invitational for Ladies at Shawnee-on-Delaware, Pennsylvania is reputed to have hit 166 strokes for the 130-yard par-three, 16th hole. Her tee shot went into the Binniekill River, and the ball floated downstream. She put out in a boat with her husband and eventually caught up to her ball 1.5 miles away. She had to play through the woods to get back.
- Arthur Thompson is reputed to have been the oldest person ever to match or better his age. He was 102 when he shot 102 at the Victoria Uplands course in Victoria, Canada.
- David B. Mulligan joined the Winged Foot Golf Club in 1937. He routinely took a second drive after duffing his first. Thus, the "Mulligan."
- In 1955, Mike Souchak shot 60-68-64-65 for a PGA Tour record 27-under-par, 257, for 72 holes, at Brackenridge Park Golf Championship in the Texas Open. The record still stands.

Highest stroke totals for a single one hole:

- 23: Tommy Armour in the 1927 Shawnee Open
- 21: Philippe Porquier in the 1978 French Open
- 19: Ray Ainsley in the 1938 U.S. Open
- 18: John Daly in the 1998 Bay Hill Invitational

42

25 Great Quotes About Golf

Few games elicit the full range of commentary, wit, and wisdom like golf. Folks from poets to presidents have had something to say about it. You can find collections of these all over the Internet, and a wonderful collection in Colin Jarman's book, *The Hole Is More than the Sum of the Putts*. This list is a small collection of favorites.

1. "Golf is an ineffectual attempt to direct an uncontrollable sphere into an inaccessible hole with instruments ill-adapted to the purpose." **—Sir Winston Churchill**

2. "Play the shot you can play best, not the shot that would look the best if you could pull it off." **—Harvey Penick**

3. "Golf tips are like aspirin. One may do you good, but if you swallow the whole bottle, you will be lucky to survive." **—Harvey Penick**

4. "I played Civil War golf; I went out in 61 and came back in 65."
—Henny Youngman

5. "The reason the pro tells you to keep you head down is so you can't see him laughing." **—Phyllis Diller**

6. "Golf...is not a particularly natural game. Like sword-swallowing, it has to be learned." **—Brian Swarbrick, *A Duffer's Guide to Golf***

7. "One of the advantages of bowling over golf is you seldom lose a bowling ball." **—Don Carter**

8. "Baseball reveals character; golf exposes it." —Ernie Banks

9. "I guess there is nothing that will get your mind off everything like golf will. I have never been depressed enough to take up the game, but they say you get so sore at yourself that you forget to hate your enemies." —Will Rogers

10. "Golf courses are built by men, but God provides the venues."
    —Robert Trent Jones

11. "I was interested in one thing—majors—because I know they live long. You could win a million dollars, and that will go. But when you win the U.S. Open or the British Open or the Masters or the PGA, the title goes to your grave." —Gene Sarazen

12. "There were three things in the world that he held in the smallest esteem: slugs, poets, and caddies with hiccups."
    —P.G. Wodehouse, *Rodney Fails to Qualify*

13. "Jackie Gleason's such a generous guy that he donated a sweater to charity as a pro-am prize, and now there's a family of refugees living in it." —Bob Hope

14. "When I tee the ball where I can see it, I can't hit it. And when I put it where I can hit it, I can't see it."
    —Jackie Gleason (on his own girth)

15. "After an abominable round of golf a man is known to have slit his wrists with a razor blade and, having bandaged them, to have stumbled into the locker room and inquired of his partners, 'What time tomorrow?'" —Alistair Cooke

16. "At golf you've got to be mentally alert. You can't lean against a tree that isn't there." —Doug Sanders

17. "Competitive golf is played mainly on a five-and-a-half-inch course: the space between your ears." —Bobby Jones

18. "Golf does strange things to other people, too. It makes liars out of honest men, cheats out of altruists, cowards out of brave men, and fools out of everybody." —Milton Gross

19. "The golf swing is like a suitcase into which we are trying to pack one too many items." —John Updike

20. "My swing is so bad, I look like a caveman killing his lunch."
    —Lee Trevino

21. "My best score ever was 103, but I've only been playing 15 years."

   —Alex Karris

22. "Golf is a game in which you yell 'fore,' shoot six, and write down five." **—Paul Harvey**

23. "Golf and sex are about the only things you can enjoy without being good at it." **—Jimmy Demaret**

24. "This hole right here can have a par of anything you want it to be. Yesterday it was a par 47—and I birdied the sucker."

   —Willie Nelson

25. "Golf is a good walk spoiled." **—Mark Twain**

43

12 Celebrities Who Play the Game

Lots of celebrities play golf, including former pro athletes, current pro athletes, and tons of actors. We all remember that Bob Hope was the king of Hollywood celebrity golfers, and Frank Sinatra and Bing Crosby were close behind him. But, here, in alphabetical order, I present a list of current celebs who play golf pretty well that just might surprise you.

1. Alice Cooper

It may seem hard to believe, but the so-called decadent rock star plays as much as five times a week. He's also a regular on the fund-raising, celebrity tournament, and stages a tournament of his own to support his Solid Rock Foundations, an organization aimed at helping inner-city kids. The man's been playing golf for nearly 20 years, and plays to a six handicap. Rock on!

2. Celine Dione

Celine is reputedly very passionate about the game. And, although she's only been at it for a few years, she's said to be quite good. She can play with me any time.

3. Kenny G

Did you know he's the best-selling instrumentalist/musician in the world? Yes, it's true. In addition to playing golf, his other hobby/passion is piloting his seaplane.

4. Dennis Hopper

If you came of age at the right time, it's a bit unnerving to think of the pot-smoking, motorcycle-jockeying guy from *Easy Rider* enjoying an afternoon on the links. But he not only came back to become a major star and film director, he also has had several gallery shows for his photography; he plays a decent game of golf, too.

5. Mickey Jones

Who's Mickey Jones, you ask? He was not only the original drummer with Bob Dylan and The Band, but was also the original drummer for Kenny Rogers and The First Edition. Indeed, according to Jones' Web site, it was Rogers who got him into golf: "Mickey recalls Kenny playing golf nearly everyday while the group was in Las Vegas. It took a lot of persuading by Kenny to get Mickey on the golf course. When Mickey finally broke down and went, he remembers that he played horrible. He did, however, have one three-wood shot that went 230 yards and that shot hooked him on golf for the rest of his life. "I love this darn game but it hates me. It is the worst narcotic I can think of, it is very addicting," Mickey says. He now plays a very consistent bogey golf—or so he claims.

6. Cheech Marin

Here's another guy who came to prominence smoking marijuana (remember *Up In Smoke?*), and who's now playing an establishment type in the television series *Nash Bridges* and living part-time in Park City, Utah. He often can be seen on the celebrity golf tournament circuit…without Chong.

7. John Cougar Mellencamp

Although he has officially dropped the "Cougar" from his name, the boy born in a small town is a golf aficionado. He was listed in the February 2001 issue of *Golf & Travel* as one of those "seen playing here" at the Daufuskie Island, South Carolina, course. The man's also a serious painter, by the way, and the profits from his book *Paintings and Reflections* (HarperPerennial, 1998), a volume of full-color reproductions, go to VH1's "Save the Music" program, which helps buy musical instruments for schoolchildren.

8. John Michael Montgomery

Can a country music twanger from Kentucky find happiness on the links? Apparently. Montgomery, who has 10 number one country singles to his credit and more than 14 million albums sold, plays to a nine handicap. He plays six tournaments annually on the Celebrity Players Tour, helping to raise money for children's charities. Y'all come out and watch him, hear?

9. Vince Neil

The man from Motley Crue has been playing for about 15 years. He claims he's not really very good, but he did once shoot a 78 at the Desert Springs Marriott, Palm Course. That's better than I ever did.

10. Jack Nicholson

It may not be a surprise that Mr. Nicholson, who may be the quintessential Hollywood guy these days, is a golfer and a good one. He's following in the Sinatra/Crosby/Hope tradition.

11. Leslie Nielsen

You have to love Leslie Nielsen. If you don't, go rent any of the *Airplane* or *Naked Gun* movies. Then go read one of his golf books: *Bad Golf My Way* (Main Street Books, 1997) or *Leslie Nielsen's Stupid Little Golf Book* (Doubleday, 1995). After that, you'll love him as an actor, writer, *and* golfer.

12. Joe Pesci

The guy from *My Cousin Vinny* and *Lethal Weapon,* a Newark, New Jersey, native, plays in celebrity fund raisers, and plays pretty well. I don't know what his handicap is, but I figure it must be pretty good. If not, he'd probably just shoot me for asking.

44

9 Ways for Non-Members to Get on a Private Course (Maybe)

As you've seen from the best courses lists, I have a definite prejudice against private clubs in favor of public ones. However, it is true that some of the world's most beautiful and challenging links are private, and many golfers spend their lives pining away for a chance to play them. Or, just pining away because they don't belong to a private club. (Remember what Groucho Marx said: "I wouldn't join any private club that would have me as a member!")

So here, after consulting Ken Beaulieu, former *Golf Player Magazine* editor and long-time editor of Continental Airlines' in-flight magazine *Continental*, inveterate golfer, and superb skier, I present some ways in which you, too, may gain entry to the tee boxes, fairways, and greens (and maybe even the club-houses, too) of private golf clubs.

1. Offer Yourself in a Trade

This works if you're already a member of a club. You can offer to trade with a member at the private course you wish to play: You play at his place, he plays at yours.

2. Check Your Own Club's Reciprocity Policy

Many clubs offer built-in reciprocity with a variety of other clubs. You may already qualify to play that fancy place on the other side of the tracks without actually knowing it.

3. Have Your Pro Contact Their Pro

Again, if you're already a member of a club, it often helps to get club pros to communicate with each other. Have your pro contact the pro at the private club of your interest and, as a courtesy to your pro, an invitation for you will likely be forthcoming. This may also work with the pro at your local public course. It's worth a try.

4. Offer Yourself Up for Charity

Many private clubs host charity golf tournaments. Sign up for one. Also, many private courses host pro tournaments, which include a charity pro-am contest. Sign up for one of those. In fact, sign up for just about anything you can think of that needs a volunteer over at the site you covet.

5. Show an Interest in Membership

Many new private courses, and some established ones with membership openings, will allow you to play a round of golf as a prospective member. (Warning! Only do this if you're seriously interested in joining, or at least can act convincingly in a way that indicates your serious interest!)

6. Shmooze the Resident Pro

Oftentimes, you can put in a call to the pro at the course you'd like to play, explain to him that you're the course's biggest fan ever and have been told repeatedly by everyone who's anyone just how fine a place it is, and he just might invite you over. In other words, shmooze him. Be sure to tell the pro you're more than willing to play when the club is least busy and that you'll pay all fees, including buying the apres-golf drinks.

7. Make Friends With Someone Who Belongs

Shmoozing a member can be just as effective as buttering up the pro. He or she just might invite you over as his or her guest. Just remember: You'll have to spend several hours with this person, so don't go playing up to jerks.

8. Become a Golf Writer

Golf writers are treated like royalty. If you can obtain a genuine, verifiable golf writer's press card, many doors just may magically open for you. (I am still working at obtaining that card, so I can't advise you on just how to obtain it or just how magical it may be.)

9. Get a Golf Industry Job

Failing all else, go to work for some company in the golf industry, which also may well open doors previously closed to the likes of you!

45

16 Surefire Practices for Lowering Your Handicap

Okay, once you're completely hooked on this game—a golf junkie of the first order—you'll soon start obsessing about your handicap. You're going to want to get it down to below sea level, submerged, or just plain eliminated. There's got to be an easy way to do this, you're thinking. But it's just not true.

There's zero substitute for practice. Well, actually, the one substitute for practice is *astute* practice. Which is to say, combining practice with lessons from a teaching pro to whom you can actually relate, one whose instruction is focused and that you understand. Here is a list of ways in which you *might* be able to lower your handicap.

1. Take Lessons

Find and work with a pro to whom you can relate.

2. Attend Golf School

Anything that says "school" may be enough to give you nightmares about failing exams. But this is actually a great way to improve your game because it allows you to undergo a number of consecutive days of intensive instruction *and* practice.

3. Buy—and Watch!—Instructional Tapes

Be careful. Everybody's got their own personal theory about how to play, and some of this stuff may not apply to you. But, if they don't work in lowering your handicap, they may work as a soporific when you can't sleep at night.

4. Read Golf Magazines

See number 3 on this list.

5. Play with Low-Handicap Golfers

As in most sports, when you play with/against guys who are better than you, your game will come up a notch or two. Don't be afraid to ask for advice during the round, but hold off on the questions while they're actually preparing a shot or swinging the club.

6. Play in a Charity Pro-Am

How else are you going to get out on the course with pros? Again, don't be afraid to ask for advice when there's no shot-making going on.

7. Try the Latest and Greatest Swing Training Gadgets

As indicated in Chapter 12, there are a lot of strange and silly gadgets out there. But some of them may actually work. Check them out and buy one or two if you think they're actually aimed at your problem(s).

8. Buy Fitted Clubs

This can be expensive, but once you've begun to play with any regularity, it's the single most effective piece of equipment advice you can take.

9. Attend Tournaments and Watch the Pros

Good technique can be contagious. Watch enough of these guys swing the club and, perhaps through osmosis, some of what they're doing right will be transmitted to you.

10. Watch Pro Tournaments on Television

See 9 on this list.

11. Play Courses from the Back Tees

This will force you to use every club in your bag, or at least *more* of those clubs you paid that small fortune for.

12. Play Early, Play Late, Play Twice

If you get out there when you can have the course to yourself (e.g., early in the morning or late in the day), you can probably play two balls. Twice the practice for one greens fee. Can it get any better than that?

13. Play More

The more you play and the more you practice, the better you will be. Maybe.

14. Get into Shape

This *is* a sport, and as in any athletics, the better your conditioning, the better you'll play. And, in this confounded game, flexibility is probably the most important element of conditioning. Of course the very idea of stretching is enough to evince incredible pain in the most horrible places. But, as in life, being flexible offers an enormous advantage.

15. Practice Course Management

Of course, you'll first have to get somebody to explain what that means, but once you know how, where, and *why* to hit the ball, this becomes a key element in your improvement.

16. Practice, Practice, Practice

And practice some more.

15 Essential Pieces of Golf Attire

Unless you're playing at a nudists' resort, you're going to need clothes for this game. Admittedly, now that tennis has come out of the white ages, this is about the only sport left that demands some kind of dress code for its practitioners. Why golfers can't play in jeans and a T-shirt is unclear, but rules are rules, as they say. It pays, by the way, to call ahead and discover any sartorial requirements held by any course you intend to play. Unless, of course, you don't mind dropping a few extra bucks at their pro shop just to be allowed onto the first tee. To develop your game properly, you'll absolutely need the items on this list.

1. Polo Shirt (Men)

This fills the old "collared shirt" rule in a comfortable way. You could conceivably show up in a dress shirt and tie, but it might constrain your swing, or your ability to relax. Polo shirts are available just about anywhere. You can pay $60 at a golf pro shop, or $8.95 at K-Mart. The choice is yours. Typical is the selection from Reebok Golf Shirts, which sell at major retailers and online for about $32.95.

2. Polo Shirt (Women)

Women must be collared as well. A major maker of women's polos is Women Bobby Jones, which sell for about $46. No matter what brand you choose, look for shirts made from soft, lightweight cotton knit with a loose, generous fit that somehow remains flattering.

The Golf Fashion Police on Patrol

3. Checked/Plaid Pants (Men only—please!)

Some folks think these are a joke. Others might think they're a cliche. But checked and plaid golf pants have been with us for as long as anyone can remember. All golfers should have a pair in their wardrobe. The only way you can do this better would be to have checked/plaid knickers. Most pro shops stock them...I think.

4. Dockers-Style Pants

Ever since Dockers brought cotton casual dress pants back from the fashion graveyard, they've been all the rage. Now that you can get them in permanent press, there's no excuse not to have a pair or two. They're good for both genders. They're comfortable and allow easy movement, which will help you swing freely. They're available in colors that will mute the ugliness of those brown-and-white, saddle-style golf shoes so many insist on wearing.

5. Bermuda Shorts (Women)

When the going really gets hot out there, any sane golfer turns to shorts—after checking with the local clothing police, of course. Bermudas are acceptable at most clubs, probably because in most styles they can be regarded as casual dress pants that have been amputated. This is another item that the frugal shopper can pick up at a discount chain like Wal-Mart, or can find from such makers as Hanasport for anywhere from $25 to $50. I prefer cotton, but you can get them in something called 100-percent polyester silk.

6. Bermuda Shorts (Men)

Just like for the ladies, Bermudas are the acceptable hot-weather wear for men. Somehow the better courses frown on cut-off jeans. Nike makes a twill version that's 100 percent cotton, and you can probably find it for $45. Wear khaki, just like everyone else. Many brands, like Arnold Palmer's, make these babies in a breathable microfiber, too, which will not only make you look cool but will keep you cool, as well.

7. Windshirt

You have to be able to take the chill off those early morning rounds or off those rounds played by the breezy seaside. The better ones are water repellant, stain repellant, and breathable. Ashworth makes one that sells for about $70. Izod makes one for women that they call "packable," which means you can stuff it into its own pocket for easy storage. It costs about $55.

8. Baseball-style Hat

Especially if you're bald(ing) and need to protect that noggin.

9. Golf Vest

Fleece vests are all the rage these days, used by skiers and anyone else who wants to look cool while staying warm when it's not too cold. They're the perfect substitute for that makes-you-look-old-and-doddery sweater vest. You can get these at Sports Authority or another sporting goods chain for about $25 (especially if you get ones marketed for skiers just as the golf season is beginning). Or, you can get name brands like Nike, Ashworth, or others and pay up to $64 or more.

10. Visor

Not recommended for bald folks. But, if you want to cut sun glare without overheating your head with a full cap, this is the ticket. Some come with towel-like, cotton lining. You should pay between $6.95 and $15.

11. Rain Jacket

Some golfers don't know enough to come in out of the rain. Actually, today's breathable, waterproof fabrics (of which Gortex is probably the best known) offer terrific rain protection while keeping your body temperature where you want it to be. Look for "waterproof" rather than "water resistant." You'll pay more, but you'll stay a lot drier. Most major makers produce these things, and you can find them for as little as $30, or as much as $100 or more.

12. Golf Umbrella

Not strictly a piece of attire, but another "must" item for folks who won't come in out of the rain, or the sun, for that matter.

13. Shoes

See Chapter 10. Everybody has to have shoes. But why are most golf shoes so ugly?

14. V-Neck Sweater

For the private club member or wanna-be, this is the classic look for those cool days. Want to go whole hog with this? Lahinch makes one of Merino wool that you can get for $110 or so.

15. Socks

Yes, there are actually sock makers out there who create socks specifically for golfers. Look for ones that are well padded in the heels and reinforced in the toes, although any good athletic or walking sock will do just fine. Avoid white unless you're wearing white shoes.

The Components of a Golf Ball

Except for those balls that come in bright yellow or orange, these spheres really all look alike, don't they? But they're not. Technology, which has so much affected everything else in the world, has not left golf balls behind. There's more than meets the eye here, so here are the:

Five Requirements for Golf Ball Size and Behavior

The USGA and R&A are very persnickety about how a golf ball is to perform. For non-science guys, the very fact that they can measure for some of these qualities, such as initial velocity, is beyond the realm of understanding. But they can, and they do. Here's what's important to them:

1. Weight

All legal balls must weigh no more than 1.62 ounces. It is legal to create lighter-weght balls—and some folks do—but get even 1/100 of an ounce beyond 1.62 and you're outta there.

2. Size

Size really *is* everything. In this case not less than 1.68 inches. In diameter, that is. Again, some folks exceed the minimum, but anything smaller is verboten. It seems that a larger-than-regulation golf ball might just be a bit easier to hit, but who on Earth would want one that was *smaller* than regulation?

3. Initial Velocity

Who thinks of these things to measure? No ball may leave the tee at a speed greater than 250 feet per second. Otherwise, speeding tickets are issued and court appearances required. (What kind of a JUGS gun can measure that kind of speed?)

4. Overall Distance Standard

Okay, figure out how they figured this one out. A ball is out of bounds if it travels more than 280 yards (in the air and on the ground), plus a possible 6-percent variance (296.8 yards total) when struck by a club head moving at 109 miles per hour. Not 100, mind you, but only 109. Why 109? That, apparently, is the average club head speed of the average PGA Tour player. (Who measured *that?*) Really, this is all too much.

5. Symmetry

The ball must be symmetrical. Round, that is. Can you imagine putting with an egg-shaped ball?

Now let's look at the:

Construction Elements of the Common Golf Ball

Golf balls come in two basic kinds: two-piece and three-piece, like business suits. Lately, however, some folks have begun making a four-piece ball. You just can't stop progress. Anyway, there is a very delicate balance to be struck among the center, the windings (in a three-piece ball), and the cover, contrived to optimize the ball's spin rate. It's the spin rate that controls how far/well/accurately your shot travels. Here are the major elements:

1. The Center

The center varies depending on whether the ball is two- or three-piece, and what kind of cover is used. Generally speaking, the center is a rubber or thermoplastic elastomer compound. Now, many balata-cover balls come with a liquid-filled, hollow center. Believe it or not, the liquid is made up of a combination of very common things like water and corn syrup. Solid rubber centers are more generally used in Surlyn-covered wound balls. The solid center is not just some ordinary rubber, of course, but an exacting brew of natural and synthetic rubbers cured by chemical reaction. Why can't these chemo-whizzes cure the common cold?

2. The Mid-Ball

Only three-piece balls have a mid-section. It's made of wound thread. (Remember unraveling baseballs and golf balls when you were a kid? Hours of unmitigated fascination and fun!) The threads are made of various rubberized materials, varying in size and wound to precise tensions.

3. The Cover

The two major cover types are balata and Surlyn. Balata is actually a certain kind of natural rubber, but nobody uses natural materials anymore, and today's balata is purely synthetic. Balata-covered wound balls give you a very soft feel. They're also reputed to yield better control, all because the balata is relatively soft and it compresses when impacted by the club face. The impact/compaction combo yields a high spin rate, which translates for some reason into better control.

Surlyn is, today, the most prevalent choice for covers. It's a thermoplastic resin that provides much better cut and abrasion resistance than balata. Surlyn, by the way, is a trademarked resin developed by the DuPont Company. Another bit of good news about Surlyn is that it can be produced in a range of hardness and flexibility, so you can get Surlyn-covered balls that lend themselves to high spin and soft feel, or others that boast low spin and longer distance.

Elastomer is a relatively new cover kid on the block. It's supposed to give you the feel and spin of balata and the durability of Surlyn.

4. Four-part construction

This is the latest concept. It has a dual core. One core, the second-from-center layer, is made of a balata and titanium mix, and the center core is of synthetic rubber.

No matter what kind of ball you use or how it was constructed, when you hit it into the water or the woods it will be lost. Which, in the end, makes all balls equal.

10 Outstanding Golf Merchants Who Sell by Catalog

Everybody loves catalogs. Even if they never get used for more than bathroom reading, they make terrific time passers or curiosity quenchers. Sometimes you even find great things to order. The best part, naturally, is that you don't have to actually go out to a store and shop. Just call in and order. Here's a list of catalogs. There's bound to be something here that appeals to you.

1. Jazz Golf

Sells distinctly styled golf equipment for all levels and ages of player.

- Address: Jazz Golf
                 300-70 Arthur St.
                 Winnipeg, R3B 1G7, Canada
- Phone: 800-336-3036 x235 or 204-947-0645 x235
- Web site: *www.jazzgolf.com*
- Catalog Cost: Free

2. The Women's Golf Catalog

As the name implies, this golf catalog is about and for women. You'll find clothing, accessories, jewelry, footwear, gifts, novelties, golf bags, and equipment.

- Address: Women's Golf Catalog
              Box 222
              Arlington, VT 05252
- Phone: 800-984-7324 or 802-447-7795
- Web site: *www.womensgolf.com*
- Catalog price: Free

3. Official PGA Tour Catalog

If you want to make like a pro, or celebrate the pro tour, this one's for you. They stock all kinds of merchandise, accessories, clothing, travel accessories, home or office decor, and even golf clubs.

- Address: Official PGA Tour Catalog
              PO Box 19987
              Birmingham, AL 35219-0987
- Phone: 888-713-8687 or 205-917-2076
- Web site: *www.pgatourshop.com*
- Catalog price: Free

4. Golfsmith Clubheads Components Catalog/ Golfsmith Accessories

Golfsmith is probably the definitive component house for golf-club making and do-it-yourself club makers. You'll find a huge variety of clubheads, shafts, and so forth. The accessories catalog is equally wide ranging, covering everything from shoes, hats, and gloves to tees, balls, ball markers, clubs, complete club sets, bags, and books.

- Address: Golfsmith Clubheads and Components Catalog
                11000 N. IH-35
                Austin, TX 78753
- Phone: 800-815-3873 or 512-837-4810
- Web site: *www.golfsmith.com*
- Catalog price: Free

5. Par Excellence Catalog

A full line of apparel, gifts, accessories, jewelry, travel bags, gadgets, and even magnetic therapy items.

- Address: Par Excellence Catalog
                12-130 Matheson Blvd. E.
                Mississauga, ON L4Z 1Y6 Canada
- Phone: 800-561-4653 or 905-502-6536
- Web site: *www.golfinn.com*
- Catalog price: Free

6. Tuttle Golf Collection

Distinctive sportswear for men and women. Very high quality. *Very* expensive.

- Address: Tuttle Golf Collection
                PO Box 888
                Wallingford, CT 06492-0888
- Phone: 800-854-3437
- Web site: *www.tuttlegolf.com*
- Catalog price: Free

7. Le Green Book 2000—American Golf

Tout pour le golf! A French-language company that offers everything from equipment and clothes to travel and course information. You can practice your French while reading it. Tres bon!

- Address: Le Green Book 2000—American Golf
             14 Rue du Regard
             75006, Paris, France
- Phone: 01 45 49 12 52
- Web site: *www.americangolfparis.com*
- Catalog price: Free

8. One Up Golf Direct

Another catalog that specializes in a full range of attire and accessories, only this one comes with a British bent.

- Address: One Up Golf Direct
             PO Box 5825
             Syston, Leicester, LE7 3YT UK
- Phone: 0116 269 6166
- Web site: *www.oneupgolf.co.uk*
- Catalog price: Free

9. House of Tees

A catalog that specializes in personalized golf tees. We all need some of those.

- Address: House of Tees
             2 Spruce St., PO Box 5000
             Dover, NJ 07801
- Phone: 800-832-5457 or 973-328-7114
- Web site: *www.golfteehouse.com*
- Catalog price: Free

10. Country Club Editions

If you think of golf as an art, or if it brings out the artist in you, these folks sell golf prints, photos, and sculptures, including arty renditions of famous golf courses from around the world and legends of the game.

- Address: Country Club Editions
                  203 DeKalb St.
                  Bridgeport, PA 19405
- Phone: 800-356-4539 or 610-279-9880
- Web site: *www.golfpix.com*
- Catalog price: Free

References

You don't come up with a book of lists without reading myriad books, talking to innumerable people, and in today's world, rifling through a billion Web sites. The following are counted among the resources that made compiling this book possible.

Books

- Booth, Alan, and Michael Hobbs. *The Sackville Illustrated Dictionary of Golf.* London, England: Sackville Books, 1987.
- Dobereiner, Peter. *The Book of Golf Disasters.* New York: Atheneum, 1983.
- ——. *Down the Nineteenth Fairway: A Golfing Anthology.* New York: Atheneum, 1983.
- Grimsley, Will. *Golf: Its History, People, and Events;* Englewood Cliffs, N.J.: Prentice-Hall, 1966.
- Jarman, Colin M. *The Hole Is More Than the Sum of the Putts: Ultimate Golf Quotations.* Chicago: Contemporary Books, 1999.
- Loeffelbein, Bob. *Offbeat Golf.* Santa Monica: Santa Monica Press, 1998.

- Mastronia, Nick. *The Insider's Guide to Golf Equipment.* New York: The Berkley Publishing Group, 1997.
- Mintzer, Rich, and Peter Grossman. *The Everything Golf Book.* Holbrook, Mass.: Adams Media Corporation, 1997.
- Penick, Harvey with Bud Shrake. *Harvey Penick's Little Red Book.* New York: Simon & Schuster, 1992.
- Player, Gary. *The Complete Golfer's Handbook.* New York: The Lyons Press, 1999.
- Steel, Donald. *Golf Facts and Feats.* Enfield, Middlesex, England: Guinness Superlatives, 1980.

Web Sites

- *Amazon.com*
- *Duffersonline.com*
- *Findgolfstuff.com*
- *Golf.com*
- *Golf-Gadgets.com*
- *Golfandtravel.com*
- *Golfballs.com*
- *Golfcourse.com*
- *Golfeurope.com*
- *Golflink.com*
- *Golfoneline.com*
- *Yahoo.com*
- *About.com*

Institutions/Organizations

- Barnes & Noble Bookstore, Paramus, New Jersey
- LPGA Tour
- Maurice M. Pine Public Library, Fair Lawn, New Jersey
- Paramus Public Library, Paramus, New Jersey
- PGA Tour
- United States Golf Association

People

- Ken Beaulieu
- Jim Gregory
- Penny Kaplan
- Mike Lewis
- Sean Mulready
- Rob Neswick
- Larry Olmsted
- Lynn Zeemont
- Dave Zeemont

Index

Y

youngest golfers to win PGA
tournaments, 93-94

Z

Zaharias, Babe Didriksen, 99-100

About the Author

Mitch Kaplan has been covering adventure and family travel for more than 10 years. An avid and fully addicted skier, he recently took up golf to fill the boringly balmy summer days between snow seasons. He currently holds the unofficial New Jersey *and* Oregon state records for most golf balls lost in a 12-hole round.

Kaplan has written *52 New Jersey Weekends, The Weekend Athlete's Injury Guide, 535 Wonderful Things to Do This Weekend,* and *The Unofficial Guide to the Mid-Atlantic with Kids,* and he co-authored *The Summer Garden Cookbook.* His work has appeared in *Skiing, Snow Country, Golf Player, Family Circle, Continental Airlines Magazine, Tower Airlines Magazine,* and *Westways,* and it can also be found on numerous Web sites.

He lives in suburban northern New Jersey with his non-skiing/non-golfing wife Penny, two college-age children who won't empty the nest, and a gorgeous mutt named Callie.